BLOODY SUMMER

Bloody Summer

George G. Gilman

NEW ENGLISH LIBRARY

TIMES MIRROR

for
V.B.
a man from out of the Northlands

An NEL Original
© George G. Gilman 1973

*

FIRST NEL PAPERBACK EDITION SEPTEMBER 1973
Reprinted April 1974

NEL Books are published by
New English Library Limited from Barnard's Inn, Holborn, London E.C.1.
Made and printed in Great Britain by Hunt Barnard Printing Ltd., Aylesbury, Bucks.

450015475

CHAPTER ONE

COLONEL George P. Haven of the 5th United States Cavalry
ran a dirt-grimed finger under the leather chin-strap of his
forage cap and rubbed off the sweat with his thumb. Then
he raised his ample rump from the non-regulation Sioux
frame saddle and massaged the chafed area. Neither act did
much to relieve the discomfort of the long ride but a man
could not ignore his own distress.

He pulled the cap peak lower on his broad forehead and
screwed up the heavily scored skin around his eyes to stare
ahead. He saw nothing more than the vista which had been
present for the past many hours. Just the buttes, canyons
and multi-coloured rock formations of clay and sand washed
from the Black Hills to the north. Perhaps the structure of
the barren landscape had altered over the miles and the
shadows had lengthened with the sun's slide towards the
western horizon: but there was nothing more definite than
this. No sudden coming upon a landmark which would tell a
man he had achieved the target of a hard day's travel.

Haven sighed and settled back into the saddle. He had
been told about the Badlands of Dakota but had never
imagined the vast scale of the country. He checked the time
shown by his gold watch and then glanced ahead again,
fixing his sights upon the mouth of a canyon which seemed
to slant south-west from the route he was taking. His evenly
tanned, clean-shaven face became set in a resolute expression
as he determined to reach the canyon before the leading arc
of the sun touched the ragged top of a butte south of his
target.

He glanced over his shoulder, at the short column of
wagons and mounted escort. His voice, rich with the brogue
of Boston-Irish, rang out clearly across the creaking of the

wagons and scraping of hooves against the sun-baked ground. 'Step it up, men. A bottle of claret for every third man if we reach sheltered ground before the sun touches the horizon.'

He raised and massaged himself once more before clucking encouragement to his chestnut mare and urging the horse into a trot.

The detachment of nine troopers – six riding as mounted escorts and three driving the covered wagons – matched the officer's pace, making sure Haven did not see the reluctance with which they followed his order. It was the driver of the last wagon in the column, out of earshot of the Colonel, who voiced the feelings of many of the men.

'I hope that Indian saddle scrapes every bit of rich hide off his smart ass,' the hawk-faced youngster growled to the mounted escort on his left.

The soured veteran spat into the rising dust. 'Good chance it will,' he answered. 'Haven ain't been sitting in anything but nice soft armchairs since he was passed out of West Point.'

This was not true. The Colonel had, as a captain, seen active duty in several major campaigns during the War Between the States and was promoted to higher ranking after the bitter Battle for Atlanta. But he was not given to boasting and in the post-war years it was inevitable that the safe and easy commands he was allotted and the comfortable life-style he adopted should give rise to a reputation he made no attempt to dispel.

He had never seen a shot fired in anger since before Appomattox. Promoted to Colonel, he had commanded a number of forts throughout the Department of the West and it was through no fault of his that Indian trouble always broke out either before he arrived in a new area or after he left. This reflected well upon him in far off Washington where luck was ruled out and he was regarded as an officer who could be trusted to keep any situation under control.

But to the men serving under him he was known as a desk-bound spit-and-polish officer. Because of Haven's

6

innate good fortune which kept trouble constantly at bay the soldiers in his command were virtually denied the justification for their existence. With no active duties to perform, and stationed in remote outposts where the monotony was only ever broken by the arrival of new supplies, the men failed to spot a dangerous enemy. But Haven recognised boredom for what it was and used the only method available to him to combat it.

Thus, the forts and men under Haven's command became models of army discipline. The routine of patrols, parades, inspections and fatigue duties were carried out strictly by the book: but were ordered with a far greater frequency than regulations specified. This meant that men who had every reason to expect an easy tour of duty away from the rigors of a front line unit found themselves caught up in a round of daily chores superintended with a harsher eye for detail than they had ever experienced before – even at training camp.

It was little wonder that George P. Haven was one of the most detested officers in the United States army. And the way in which he surrounded himself with the luxuries of life even at the most remote fort in the territories did little to salve the men's resentment towards him.

Nor did he forego his creature comforts on the trail so that, as soon as the small wagon train reached the cool interior of the canyon and he had selected a suitable camp-site, two men were immediately detailed to attend to Colonel Haven's needs.

While the remainder of the troopers took care of the horses and prepared a cooking fire, these two off-loaded several pieces of furniture from the lead wagon. First there was a rosewood dresser, complete with three mirrors and an inset enamel washbasin. Then an oval topped, carved oak table and matching chair from England. Finally a deep-seated fireside chair and velvet covered footstool which had been imported from France.

Haven overseed the unloading, urging care and roaring abuse whenever a piece of furniture seemed in danger of being knocked or scratched. It was all placed carefully into

7

the pattern of a makeshift room setting with the sides of the wagons serving as three walls. The fire was built in the downwind opening.

'Haven at the Badlands Ritz,' an ageing busted sergeant rasped as he lowered a wickerwork basket to the ground at one side of the fire.

The Colonel, stripped to his undervest and light blue uniform pants, was bent over the basin in the dresser, washing his face. He was probably aware of the kind of comments passed about him and sensed the hostility of his men. But he had long ago learned to accept his self-appointed role of hard taskmaster and to ignore the hatred it engendered. He even went to the lengths of turning a blind eye or a deaf ear towards the more careless taunts and punished only the most blatant acts of insubordination. For it was his philosophy that a soldier was only a good one if he had something to hate. Usually, it was a conventional enemy. So to keep his men on their mettle, in readiness for an actual enemy, he created a bogus one.

The train had reached the objective in the time set by Haven, but it was not yet sundown. Before the sun dipped into a distant range of mountains and poured a more mellow light across the Badlands outside the canyon, the camp was fully established. Haven had washed, shaved and donned a fresh uniform before the sandstone slopes of the vast wasteland were turned into a myriad shades of pink and purple and brown as the day ended.

He waited, patient and lonely, at the carefully set table, smoking a cheroot and sipping sherry from a crystal glass as the salt beef stew bubbled over the fire. The troopers who had arranged his comforts, returned to their companions and sank down to the rocky ground with sighs of relief. The younger one stretched out full length and rested the back of his head into his interlocked hands as he stared up at the clear greyness of the darkening sky.

'He's as nutty as a one-eyed loon!' the boy pronounced.

The corporal who had helped the boy attend to Haven's evening needs for the three nights out from Fort Abercrombie, nodded his agreement. The busted sergeant who was the detachment's cook on the trip, gave the stew a final stir and glared through the smoke at the officer.

'He ain't nutty,' he hissed. 'He's in this man's army because he knows he can get what he likes out of it.' He swung round to face the others, all lying or squatting on the ground, clothes still dusty and faces grimed with the dried sweat of the trail. 'Why are we in it?' he demanded.

'I dunno,' the hawk-faced driver of the last wagon admitted, and shot a glance over his shoulder, out of the mouth of the canyon towards the suddenly cold darkness of rolling barrenness. 'But I figure to stay in a while longer. That ain't friendly country out there. Sioux land.'

'Gotta be a better place to take off than in Indian territory,' a trooper with a scar over his nose pointed out.

'Proves what I said,' the boy put in. 'Man's just got to be crazy to go riding through Sioux country with his ass smoothing the hide of an Indian saddle.'

The men's conversation reached Haven as a low murmuring and he made no effort to pick out and isolate any particular phrases. He was content to pour himself a second glass of sherry and finish the cheroot; to gaze at the silver place setting reflecting the flickering firelight; to feel the crispness of the starched white linen tablecloth beneath his scrubbed fingers: to enjoy the fruits of a life earned in part by intelligent work but mostly showered upon him under the terms of his father's will.

The meal did not reach the high standards of his preparation for it. But although he expected the best from his men, he did not demand miracles. A stew cooked over a campfire was the same whether served on a plate of bone china or in a mess tin. When it had been served and a bottle of French white wine was uncorked for him, he told the boy to open a case of claret and pass out three bottles to be shared among the men.

The boy thanked the Colonel on behalf of his companions and, although the men would have preferred a single bottle of the Napoleon brandy with which Haven finished his meal, they enjoyed the gift. But since it was a small enough return for the many disagreeable tasks involved in the journey,

9

none of the men regretted that he had spat into the tureen from which the Colonel's stew was served.

Haven took his brandy, and another cheroot, relaxing in the winged chair, his booted feet resting comfortably on the stool. Eventually he would fall asleep there, lulled by the quietness of the night or perhaps by the playing of the busted sergeant's mouth organ. For as long as he stayed in the chair – maybe right through to dawn – it was necessary for the posted sentry to keep the fire blazing so that the Colonel would not wake cold. Only if something roused him and he decided to retire to his bed in one of the wagons was it permitted to let the fire die down.

Colonel Haven did not go to bed that night and it was the roaring fire, lighting up the mouth of the canyon like a yellow signal beacon, which drew the attention of Tom and Ed Ball and the four men who rode with the brothers.

The Ball gang were two days hard riding out of Deadwood and had been able to make good time because they were not weighed down by the rich proceeds of an express office robbery that went wrong. For half the first day they had been glad they were travelling light: the gap which their speed opened up between themselves and the sheriff's posse dissuading the lawman and his deputies from continuing the fruitless chase.

But even when the gang was out of the Black Hills, Tom Ball kept the pace hot. It was a long way home and after the Deadwood job going wrong he was not anxious to pull anything else without careful planning. He found it much easier to work things out when he was holed up in the safety of the gang's permanent hide out: and from the mood of his brother and the others it was apparent that he would have to stage something soon if he wanted to stay the top man.

So he pushed them hard and he was so intent upon considering the possibilities of the horses being run out before the end of the trip that he failed to see the firelight of the camp before the others spotted it. The six men reached the top of a smooth crested rise in a group and Tom, in the lead, was several yards down the other side before he realised the others had reined in their horses.

He halted his own mount and stared back up the slope anxiously. Then he forced his stubbled features to form a snarl and his voice was as hard as the rock beneath him. 'We'll do the moonlight sightseeing tour another time!'

'Company ahead, Tom,' Ed answered, pointing.

Tom had to heel his horse back up the slope to see over the brow of the next rise to where the wagon trains' fire sent suffused light from out of the canyon's mouth. He halted beside his brother and it was only at such times, when the two men were close together, that the family connection was evident. At thirty-two, Tom was the senior by ten years. His stature of six feet made him the taller by half a foot. Both had pale green eyes beneath low foreheads and a line of mouth which suggested a generosity betrayed by their natures. But these common features were not predominantly apparent when the two were apart and the leanness of Tom's face was in marked contrast to the bloated cheeks and double chins of his brother. This difference – slimness against obesity – extended to the contrasting builds of the two men and was caused by Ed's sweet-tooth for candy.

'Could be Indians,' Tom said after a few moments for thought, blowing on his hands and turning up the collar of his fur-lined jacket. 'We'll give 'em a wide berth.'

Grant Kelton shook his head and stroked his drooping moustache. 'Ain't nothing for the Sioux in these parts. Ain't hunted this part of back of beyond for years.'

Sam Lambert and Pete Bean nodded their agreement. Lee Bolan slid his Winchester from its boot and pumped a shell into the breech. Then he put it back and rubbed his hands together.

'Cold night,' the poker-faced Bolan commented. 'Even if the horses kept stood up for the rest of it, don't reckon we'll get where we're going by morning.'

'Fire sure does look good, Tom,' Ed said, giving his brother a sidelong glance, a half smile turning up the corners of his mouth.

'We can light our own fire,' Tom shot back, sensing the eyes of the other four men were upon the brothers.

11

None of the quartet was capable, or even inclined, to take over leadership of the gang. They were prepared to follow whoever made the plans that kept the loot coming. But Tom had slipped up on the Deadwood robbery and that left him wide open to be dethroned. They all knew Ed had been itching for a long time to do things his way.

'Ain't never so warm as one somebody else lit,' Ed pressed, his tone easy. 'I reckon we ought to go take a look.'

'So why don't you,' Tom rasped. 'But if that's a Sioux fire and you get too close, you just might find out how warm it really is.'

'I'm with Ed,' Kelton said as the younger brother heeled his horse down the incline.

'Me, too,' Lambert put in, moving forward and checking the action of his Colt .45 as he fell into line behind the others.

'Don't reckon them's Injuns, Tom,' Pete Bean said thoughtfully. 'And if they ain't, they might just be able to help cut our losses on the Deadwood foul up.'

Bolan moved up alongside Bean without a word and both heeled their mounts to catch up with the others.

Tom felt the anger building up inside him and his right hand dropped to the butt of the holstered Remington .36 five-shot which jutted out from under his jacket. But rage was as futile as the revolver against these men – unless he was prepared to use it effectively. So he steeled himself against his impulse and heeled his horse savagely to drive the animal down towards the others. The five had bunched up into a group again and they eyed Tom with cool indifference as he forced a way through them.

'Okay,' he yelled. 'You want to make a dumb move, I'll go along. But somebody else is going to do the figuring. It blows up in your faces, it's nothing to do with me.'

His angry outburst was greeted with an uncaring silence which was punctured at length by a snort from Bean's horse.

'I couldn't have put it better myself, Tom,' Ed said softly, his fleshy face set in a self-satisfied smirk.

Tom glared at him but held his peace, suddenly aware of

the possible consequences of handing over the initiative to his brother. All Ed needed was a lucky break and he would have proved himself. It was something he had wanted to try for a long time and if he once tasted success, there would be no holding him. The streak of viciousness that Tom had always suspected was in Ed would come to the surface and lash out. And if the kid's luck held it could set the territory alight and keep it burning for as long as the breaks stayed with him.

When the group crested the next rise they were much closer to the glow but still far enough away to fail to distinguish any figures within range of the firelight.

'Sioux wouldn't light a fire big as that,' Kelton said with soft-voiced conviction. 'Injuns might be crazy in the head, but they know better than to tell everyone within a hundred miles where they're resting up for the night.'

Although he did not voice it, Tom Ball agreed with Kelton. He had known from the very moment he saw the fire that it had not been lit by Sioux. But it had been worth trying to scare the men away. The ruse had failed and now Tom found himself involved in an impulsive non-plan to move in on whoever was camped in the canyon mouth. It was so much against his nature – and against his methods which had always worked perfectly until Deadwood – that Tom had to hold himself back from angling his horse away from the group. It was only the long-ago promise to a dying father that he would take care of his kid brother that kept Tom in his place, to the left and slightly behind Ed.

So much of his concentration was directed inwardly, Tom failed to catch the first part of what Ed was saying. But the kid captured the attention of the hard-eyed men, who listened like deeply engrossed children to a new teacher yet to prove himself. But Tom heard enough to realise exactly what the plan entailed. He swung his eyes along the faces of the men, desperate to spot some sign that they would not go through with it. But he saw only tacit approval of what Ed wanted: and in some cases the glinting of an eye or the licking of a lip betrayed a mounting excitement held in check.

'Ed, that's –' Tom started.

'I know what it is,' Ed snapped, his voice filled with a sudden cold anger. 'It's my way. You struck out back there and now it's my turn. Only the game's changed. If you don't like it, the ball park's due east from here. But we been away a long time and it'll be cold. We figure to warm us before we make a home run.'

Again, the five riders moved on ahead of Tom, angling away to the side so that they would not approach the canyon mouth from the exposed front. Tom held back for only a few moments before going forward to rejoin them.

Following Ed's instructions, they dismounted a hundred yards from their objective and drew the Winchesters and Springfields from their saddle boots.

'We need someone to hold the horses,' Ed whispered, looking pointedly at his brother.

The others glanced in the same direction and when Tom failed to reply, each man passed his reins to the deposed leader. Tom accepted them and cleared his throat. 'Anything could happen in there.'

Ed's puffy face showed a grin but his whispered voice was charged with evil. 'Right, Tom. But be sure you hang around to find out what. We have to leave in a hurry, we want to find the horses ready and waiting.'

The others treated Tom to a series of steady, hard-eyed stares before moving off in the wake of Ed, the group becoming silhouetted against the fire's glow for a few moments. Then they were lost against the deep shadows of the canyon wall.

Colonel Haven snored gently in the deep-seated armchair, his smooth-shaven face ruddy from the heat of the fire. He was not armed. Eight of his men were sprawled out under blankets on the far side of the fire. The ninth trooper – the boy who was so convinced his commanding officer was mad – sat hugging his knees, a blanket draped over his shoulders. He had only recently fed fresh brush to the fire, which was consuming the kindling with an angry crackling sound. The noise covered the occasional careless footfall of the approaching men.

14

Occasionally the boy looked up, glancing across the sleeping troopers with their rifles, still in the shoulder belts, resting nearby. Then he would stare out of the canyon into the darkness of the desolate wastes beyond. He did this merely to prevent himself dozing: nobody expected trouble but the Colonel was not the kind of officer to forego the tradition of posting sentry duties.

'Evening, soldier boy,' a voice called softly.

The young trooper snapped up his head and gasped, reaching for the Sharps carbine laid out between his feet. But he stayed his hand, every muscle in his body frozen by fear.

The five men stood in a line, with Ed Ball at the centre. It was he who had spoken and now he raised a finger to his lips, urging quiet. The muzzle of Ed's Winchester was aimed at the boy's head. The other men covered the sleeping troopers.

'Where you headed, soldier boy?' Ed asked, his voice a whisper.

The sentry made a harsh, low gurgling sound in his throat, then managed to force out the words. 'Fort Bridger, Department of Utah.'

'Payroll in the wagons?' Ed asked.

'With our luck?' Bolan muttered.

The trooper shook his head and dragged his eyes away from the intruders to glance at the cavalrymen. Not one of them even stirred in his sleep. He wondered if he would be court-marshalled. 'Personal stuff for the Colonel,' he said. 'Being shipped to a new posting.'

'Valuable?' Ed asked, his eyes greedy.

'I don't know about stuff like that,' the trooper replied.

'We're wasting time,' Pete Bean said anxiously. 'Let's do it.'

The young trooper began to sweat. Drops ran into his eyes and stung. He wanted to wipe the sweat away but couldn't. He didn't want the men to think he was crying.

'I don't go for messing around with the army,' Bolan said.

'Who'll know it was us?' Ed asked easily and shot the boy. The 44/40 bullet drilled through the youngster's right

15

eye and spewed blood from the side of his head as he was flipped over backwards.

The eight men who had been sleeping were jerked into awareness and four died a split-second after waking, the bullets drilling into their defenceless bodies before they could move. Another trooper – a veteran of countless surprise attacks – rolled away as a reflex action and scooped up his rifle. He had a fleeting impression of a figure leaping towards him and fired. The busted sergeant took the bullet in his throat and coughed blood into the veteran's face as he fell. Kelton, Bean and Ed Ball fired simultaneously and the veteran's head exploded into fragments of blood-dripping flesh.

The eighth man died in screaming agony, a bullet from Lambert taking him in the shoulder and spinning him as he got to his feet: then Bolan's Springfield sent a non-fatal bullet into the trooper's thigh. The man, calling his wife's name, toppled into the fire, his hair and uniform bursting into flames.

The trooper with a scar over his nose drew a bead on Ed and pulled the trigger a moment after the man in the fire screamed his final breath. The metallic click was very loud in the sudden silence. Even the fire had ceased to crackle, as if content with the new taste of human flesh. The trooper stared down in horror at his useless rifle and then clawed at it with trembling fingers.

'No use, soldier,' Ed said.

The man was on his knees. He dropped the rifle and clasped his hands together. His lips moved in a silent prayer. Five rifles cracked in unison. The left side of the trooper's chest became shiny with blossoming patches of blood which merged into one enormous stain as he toppled over.

'Who'll know it was us?' Ed asked again as the men, still formed into a line, raked their eyes across the sprawled bodies of the dead troopers.

Kelton wrinkled his nose against the sweet odour of charred flesh and the biting stench of drifting gunsmoke. 'It was fun,' he said. 'But we didn't come out here for the hunting. Let's see what we got ourselves.'

16

He stepped forward, the heel of his boot cracking the bones in the outstretched hand of a dead trooper. Ed, anxious to assert his authority over the older men, moved quickly across the blood-soaked, body-strewn campsite and beat Kelton to the far side of the fire. He pulled up short, staring incredulously.

'Holy cow, will you look at that!' he exclaimed.

The others matched his expression as they saw the Colonel sitting amid his alfresco luxury. But he was no longer enjoying it. A stray bullet had passed through the leaping flames of the fire and angled into Haven's neck. Blood was still trickling from the jagged wound to stain the stiff collar of his jacket.

'Must be the guy who owns the stuff in the wagons,' Kelton growled. 'Don't reckon he needs it any more.'

Ed's fleshy face broke out into a grin 'Right, Grant,' he said, moving forward and using the stock of his Winchester to lever the inert form from the chair. He dropped down into the still warm seat. 'I guess we inherit it, uh?'

Kelton nodded and eyed the overweight youngster sourly. 'It just better be worth having, Ed,' he warned.

Bolan and Lambert had already climbed up into the rear of one of the wagons. 'Well, it sure is different,' Bolan yelled.

CHAPTER TWO

THE piebald picked his weary way among the fallen rocks at the foot of a towering butte, avoiding the patches of frozen snow which glittered in early morning sunlight. He was a game animal but worth no more than the two dollars his rider paid for him. A horse of that age could not be expected to carry a full-grown man over long stretches of winter Badlands without frequent stops for rest.

The rider realised this and was aware that the time was fast approaching when he must allow his mount another respite. He could hear the rushing sound of fast-flowing water ahead and he ran an olive skinned hand down the animal's neck: a sign that he understood his mount's distress and intended to do something about it.

The gesture was out of keeping with the appearance of the man in the saddle. He had a tall, deceptively lean frame, for his body was packed with more than two hundred pounds of weight. Of the powerful kind, with muscle allowing no room for excess fat. His face was long with the high cheekbones, flared nostrils and burnished skin-tones of a Latin ancestry. These features, together with the shoulder-length jet black hair which framed them were, in fact, the unmistakable signs of a half Mexican parentage. They had come from his father. But the eyes which surveyed the world with cool detachment from between narrowed lids were ice-blue, like arctic water in sunlight. These revealed the Scandinavian forebears of his mother. The mouth line, too, was modelled upon a European pattern, but the way in which the lips were held in a thin, straight line – ready to curl back and show gleaming teeth in an animalistic snarl – was a product of the man's own life.

For this man was the one who had come to be called Edge. And Edge was the kind of man who might show placid gentleness to his horse one moment and in the next cold-bloodedly kill a man – or woman.

He saw the woman as he rounded the butte, and reined in the horse, his right hand dropping to grip the butt of his holstered Remington. It was a reflex action at coming upon the unexpected and his coolness of mind enabled him to halt the draw. His hooded eyes raked to left and right, taking in every detail of the river bank scene, eager for a sign of danger. It looked innocent enough.

The woman was a redhead in her mid-twenties, with a pretty face still retaining the fresh bloom of youth. She was standing towards the middle of the shallow river with the crystal clear water rushing around her legs at a mid-thigh level. Her slender, high-breasted body was blue tinged with

18

the cold for she was stark naked. As Edge watched her, from a sideways on position, the firm swells of her brown crested breasts abruptly expanded with an intake of breath. Then she thrust herself down into a crouch and emitted a cry of half pain, half pleasure. The frothing water tugged at her long hair as if trying to drag her head under the surface.

The river, curving around in an arc to follow the foot of the butte before widening to meander across an undulating area of time-smoothed rock, was about twenty feet across at the point where the woman was bathing. On the far bank from where Edge watched there was a small fire with a steaming pot set amid the red embers. It gave off an appetising aroma of boiling coffee into the clear, frosty air. A horse was hobbled nearby and, closer to the fire, was a saddle and blanket roll and a heap of clothes.

A splashing sound from the river drew Edge's attention back to the woman and he saw her try to stand up. She was almost knocked over by the swift current, but flailed her arms and managed to retain her balance.

'Can't understand why they call these the Badlands,' he said easily as he heeled his horse forward to the edge of the bank. 'Look pretty good from where I am.'

The woman swung around to face him, her eyes wide with shock. Her mouth dropped open as if she intended to scream, but no sound emerged. She was too stunned to move for a moment, but then she tried to cover herself. One hand went between her legs as she folded the other arm across her breasts.

'You –' she screamed and struggled to think of a suitable name for him.

Edge showed his teeth in an appreciative grin. 'Your arms didn't develop so well as some other parts of you, ma'am,' he pointed out.

She put both arms across her chest, realised what this meant and crouched down in the freezing water. 'Peeping Tom!' she managed to fling at him.

Edge heeled his horse forward into the river, angling across to where the woman was crouching. She gasped and thrust herself deeper, until just her head was above the

19

surface again. He halted and grinned down at her. 'You ain't really mad at me, ma'am,' he teased. 'If you were really angry you'd go red, or maybe even purple. Fact is, you're turning blue.'

'Oh, you beast!' she screamed. 'You get away from me. And you keep your back turned this way.'

'There's one thing I'd do that for,' he told her.

Her teeth were chattering and the cold was now merely painful. It showed in the green depths of her large eyes. 'I've ... I've got ... no mon ... money,' she stuttered.

Edge nodded. 'Always nice to meet a pretty woman and find out there's common ground,' he said. 'But I was thinking that right now I'd rather have a cup of hot coffee than a thousand dames with no clothes on.'

'Help your ... yourself, mister,' she said, the anger leaving her as she had to concentrate against fainting with the cold.

'Obliged,' Edge said and continued on across the river.

As he dismounted and loosened his saddle cinch, then hobbled his horse on the patch of tough grass beside the woman's mount, he heard the redhead wading ashore. He was careful to keep his back to her as he squatted close to the fire and poured the strong coffee into one of two mugs.

'I don't like being called a dame,' the woman complained suddenly, between bouts of shivering as she towelled herself down.

Edge sipped the steaming coffee, enjoying the warmth it suffused throughout his body. His hooded eyes studied the ground, close to the edge of the river where there were patches of mud. More than one horse had crossed at this point and he decided the right number was two.

'Politest name I know for a female who takes off her clothes in a public place,' he said absently, hearing the rustle of silk against skin as she pulled on her petticoats.

He looked up but within his range of vision in this direction there was only the bleak terrain of gentle rises and slopes that offered no cover in rifle range. So he turned around. The woman was in the process of putting on her dress, but she was already decently covered.

20

'Public place, my eye!' she shot back. 'You must be the only man within fifty miles of here. How was I to know you'd come lumbering by just as I was taking a bath?'

'Man's got to have some good luck sometimes,' he answered, surveying the countryside to the west.

It was much more rugged in that direction. Cliffs and outcrops of rock, with some thick brush growing in close to the river on both banks. And the morning shadow thrown by the towering butte would further aid somebody who wanted to get in close to the campsite without being seen.

'Your good luck was my bad,' she answered with a spiteful glance at him as she shrugged into a buckskin jacket, the colour matching her eyes and contrasting with the vivid red of her dress.

Edge looked at her left hand and saw no rings or marks where rings had been. 'Saving the view for someone special?' he asked.

'That's none of your business,' she snapped, and moved towards him. She crouched down and snatched up the second mug.

'Maybe,' Edge allowed, and shot a glance away from the campsite again. 'Just making conversation.'

'Well make it about something else,' she retorted, pouring herself a mug of coffee. 'My personal life's my own.'

Edge shrugged. 'Okay. But I didn't think you'd mind telling me the secrets of your life.' He grinned. 'Considering I've seen some pretty private parts already.'

'You beast!' she shrieked, and suddenly hurled the mug of scalding coffee at him as she burst into tears.

Edge ducked to the side and heard the sizzle of liquid in the fire. The viciousness which a violent life had injected into his bloodstream welled up inside him. The woman was rooted to the spot by fear as she saw the slitted eyes and the thin gleam of his teeth between drawn back lips.

'I'm sorry!' she rasped, clasping her throat with both hands.

The mean streak that was always just below the surface shell of Edge broke through into an act of hate as he raised his hand to launch a powerful blow that might have broken

21

the woman's neck. But the sharp crack of the rifle shot blasted a hole in Edge's anger. Sparks showered up from where the bullet penetrated the embers.

'John!' the woman breathed, relief flooding strength into her muscles so that she was able to scamper away from Edge.

'He the one?' Edge asked softly, turning his head to pick out the sharpshooter.

'No,' the woman gasped. 'My brother.'

Edge, his anger dead, his brain working coolly again, clicked his tongue against the roof of his mouth. 'A brother can be worse,' he murmured.

The rifleman emerged from the deep shadow of the butte. He sat astride a tall chestnut stallion which he guided across the river with his knees. Both hands were occupied with a bolt-action Remington-Keene repeater which was aimed steadily at Edge's chest as the half-breed rose to his feet.

'Do I have reason to kill him, Elizabeth?' the rifleman asked as he came clear of the river and slid smoothly from the saddle, without using his hands or allowing his aim to waver.

'My goodness, no!' the woman said hurriedly.

The two men surveyed each other across ten feet of clear morning air. Edge saw a man of about his own age, but a good three inches shorter and more slightly built. The woman had collected all the good looks in the family and her brother had a homely, long-nosed, sunken-cheeked face. His eyes were the same attractive colour as his sister's, but spaced too closely together and were too small. He was dressed, like Edge, in a fur-lined jacket and denim pants tucked into riding boots. But instead of a low-crowned, wide-brimmed hat he wore an old fashioned trapper's hat of fur. Thin red hair poked out over his ears. His smooth hands and pale complexion marked him as a man away from his element out here in the wilderness of the Dakotas. But his skilled horsemanship, accuracy with a rifle and the firmness with which he kept Edge covered warned the half-breed that this was no tenderfoot.

'What do you want here, mister?' he asked.

'Rest up my horse and have a cup of coffee,' Edge replied easily. 'Seems you and your sister staked first claim to this spot. She invited me to stay.'

John shot a quizzical glance towards his sister and Edge felt confident enough to let the mistake pass.

The woman hesitated a moment, but finally supplied the right answer. 'That's right, John. He just arrived out of nowhere and asked for some coffee. I didn't see any harm.'

John's expression did not soften. 'What started the argument?'

Again the woman paused before replying and when Edge looked at her he saw she was suddenly wearing an expression of coyness. Then she looked down at the ground and began to finger the buttons on her jacket. 'I think the gentleman misinterpreted something I said, John,' she replied contritely.

'I keep telling you about the way you talk to strange men, Elizabeth,' John said, then sighed and abruptly lowered the rifle, an amiable smile spreading across his face. 'I must apologise for my sister, Mr . . .'

'Edge,' the half-breed supplied impassively as John approached him with an outstretched hand.

'Edge?' John tried tentatively, then shrugged. 'She's something of an innocent, I'm afraid. Led rather a sheltered life. Inclined to be over-trusting.'

'Runs in the family,' Edge said as he grasped the proffered hand, swung it to the side, then up.

John yelled in pain and whirled around, putting his back to Edge as his forearm was forced up into a painful hammerlock.

'Drop the rifle, John,' Edge whispered in his ear, so close the helpless man could feel the warmth of the half-breed's breath.

The rifle clattered to the hard ground and Edge pushed the man away from him with a violent shove before stooping to retrieve the weapon.

'Hold it right there, mister!' Elizabeth yelled, bringing a hand out of her jacket pocket. Her shaking fist was folded around the butt of a Ladies Companion six-shot pepperbox.

Edge sighed. 'Innocent is right,' he said to John, who was rubbing his pained arm.

'Don't be ridiculous, Elizabeth,' John chided his sister. 'Even if you could hit him from that range you'd probably only bruise him.'

Elizabeth's resolute determination suddenly evaporated and she stared down at the tiny gun in her hand. 'Oh my,' she exclaimed.

Edge picked up the Remington rifle and held it loosely at his side, pointed at the ground. He looked at the woman expectantly.

'Why did you give it to me then?' she demanded of John angrily. 'What's the use of a gun that's no good.'

John glanced at Edge and swallowed hard. 'It's for self-defence at short range, Liz,' he said, slowly and distinctly, as if talking to a slow-witted child. 'A man has to be more or less standing right beside you before it would do any good.'

'Oh my,' Elizabeth repeated and hurriedly thrust the tiny weapon back into her pocket. But suddenly she sought to re-assert her anger. She glared at Edge. 'That wasn't very nice – what you did to John.'

'I'm not a very nice guy,' Edge told her, and squatted down to pour himself another cup of coffee. 'I'm especially un-nice when a dame tries to scald me and a guy take pot-shots at me. But I'm a lot easier to get along with when I hold all the cards. That thing in your pocket is just a joker.'

He sipped the coffee, seeming to ignore the brother and sister. Elizabeth scratched her head and looked at John, who shrugged and winced as the gesture hurt his arm. Then the woman abruptly thudded a fist into an open palm.

'I know what you are!' she exclaimed. 'You're headed for Summer, right?'

Edge eyed her quizzically across the chipped rim of the mug. 'I didn't know you could head for it,' he replied. 'Figured it just naturally followed spring.'

'Don't pretend,' she rebuked him. 'You know I mean the town of Summer.'

Edge turned up the collar of his jacket and nodded

reflectively. 'It has a nice warm sound to it. Maybe I'll drop by.'

Elizabeth smiled triumphantly. 'You can't fool me, mister. You've got the look of the gunslinger about you. Hasn't he got the look of the gunslinger, John?'

It was an idea that didn't appeal to John. He tried to belittle it. 'When did you ever see a gunslinger, Liz?' he asked with a laugh that lacked humour.

It halted the woman, but only momentarily. 'He just looks like one, that's all,' she pronounced with feminine logic.

'That where you're heading?' Edge asked, addressing John.

He nodded and glared fleetingly at his sister. 'And we certainly aren't gunslingers.'

Elizabeth stamped her foot in irritation and swung her back towards the men.

Edge finished his coffee and stood up. 'What makes Summer a centre of attraction?' he asked in a tone which suggested he was indifferent to whether or not he got an answer.

John realised that Edge really was ignorant of the significance of the town. 'For you – and anybody else who's interested – a chance to earn ten thousand dollars reward money,' he said.

Edge's air of detachment left him. He saw the woman move and swung towards her. But she had merely crossed to her horse and was swinging the saddle across the animals' back.

'I checked at the sheriff's office in the last town I passed through,' Edge said, returning his cold gaze to John. 'Ain't no wanted men in this area worth that kind of bounty.'

John shook his head. 'Private reward. It's been put up by a man named George P. Haven for the return of some property that was stolen from him.'

Edge spat into the fire. 'You and your quick-draw side-kick figure to chance your luck against the kind of men a reward that big will bring in?'

An expression that was a mixture of hatred and grief

showed on John's unhandsome face. 'Elizabeth and I have private business in Summer.'

The woman swung up into the saddle and shot a haughty look at Edge. 'Did you find the place, John?' she asked.

'I found it,' he replied. 'A mile or so along the course of the river, then a couple of miles to the north.'

Sadness showed in the depths of her eyes and when she became aware that Edge was witnessing the emotion, she turned away. 'Come on then. I'm anxious to see it.'

John waited for Edge to move away, crossing to his horse to tighten the cinch. Then he crouched down to smother the fire and gather up the coffee pot and mugs. He pushed them into his blanket roll and he and Edge mounted together.

'Here!' the half-breed called and tossed the man's rifle back to him.

John caught the weapon and slid it into his saddle boot with smooth expertise.

'How extremely generous of you, Mr Edge,' Elizabeth said with heavy sarcasm.

'I figure I can pick the right people to trust,' he told her. 'And folks that ride together should trust each other.'

'You're coming to Summer with us?' John asked, surprised.

'You told me ten thousand good reasons why I should,' Edge answered.

'A gunslinger, I told you,' the woman said with a smirk as she heeled her horse forward, leading the way along the course of the rushing river.

'Glad to have your company,' John said, as if he meant it.

Edge showed him a gold grin. 'Just look upon it as a birthday present,' he said.

Elizabeth looked sharply over her shoulder.

John furrowed his brow. 'Both our birthdays are months off, Mr Edge,' he said.

'Ma'am, you were just trying to confuse me with that pretty suit I saw,' Edge drawled to the woman.

Her features were suddenly suffused by a pink glow. 'Oh my!' she shrieked and dug in her heels hard, spurring the horse into a gallop which shot her far ahead of the two men.

'Suit?' John asked in confusion.

'Cute little double-breasted number,' Edge replied, urging his own mount into a gallop.

CHAPTER THREE

WHEN the trio of riders rounded the western face of the butte they saw another panorama of undulating wasteland. A harsh wind from out of the far distant Black Hills, spotted with cold drops of rain, gusted at them spitefully as they broke cover.

Edge stood in his stirrups and jammed his hat on hard against the tug of the wind as he surveyed the territory ahead. The river narrowed suddenly and cut forcefully through smooth-sided gullies bare of vegetation as it swung in from the north. The ground rose almost imperceptibly in solid waves in that direction while to the west and south it was featured with grotesque formations of ancient rock around which the wind made strange sounds likes the howls of many wounded animals.

'It's eerie,' Elizabeth said with a shudder, peering out between the waves of her red hair which the wind tossed across her face. 'It's like the wailing of the ghosts of all the men who have died in this God-forsaken place.'

Edge settled back into his saddle and looked across at John, seeing the very deep and very private sorrow in the man's eyes. 'You scouted this area awhile back?'

John nodded absently.

'I don't see any signs of a town,' Edge told him.

'Summer's a long way from here,' the woman explained. 'John was looking for the trail.'

Edge signalled for John to lead the way and he did so, keeping to the water course for over two miles, moving directly into the full angry force of the wind. They all rode with their heads down, hunched into the saddles, having to keep a tight rein on their horses as the animals showed their unwillingness to move against the elements.

'There it is,' John said suddenly, halting and pointing down at the ground.

They were at the side of a shallow basin in which the river formed a small pool, constantly filling at one side and emptying at another. It was not a point in a trail as such, but marked a resting stage for a wagon train that had broken in a new route of its own. There was a patch of blackened rock where a fire had burned; some decomposing horse droppings; ruts sunk by iron-rimmed wheels; even a few footprints baked by sun and hardened by frost and frozen snow.

Once the train – Edge figured three heavily laden wagons and any number of riders – had left the watering place, angling towards the south-west, the signs of its passing became fewer.

'We have to follow the tracks to Summer?' the half-breed asked.

'No,' John replied. 'I know where Summer is. But it's necessary for Elizabeth and I to stop off somewhere else first.'

'But not for me,' Edge said. 'With ten grand up for grabs at the end of the trip I can't afford to make any detours.'

'The place we need to visit is on the way to Summer,' John said. 'And we won't be staying long.'

'So let's not waste any more time here,' Edge said sourly and moved up out of the basin.

The others followed, content to let him do the tracking, perhaps recognising that he was more skilled in the art than either of them. The going was easier now with the wind angling in at them from behind and to their right. The wagon train had swung first one way and then the other, taking the least difficult path through the broken terrain. But, Edge realised, the overall course it was steering lay to the south-west and, as the grey storm clouds scudded across to blanket the entire sky and blot out the sun, he began to cut corners.

As he took the horses through stretches of scattered boulders wagons would be unable to negotiate and up steep inclines which the train would have had to bypass, he often lost the sign he was following. But he always picked up the traces again and after calling a halt to survey what lay ahead, he no longer bothered to track. For the south-western horizon was marked by a high bluff guarded by outposts of monolithic buttes and pillars of rock. The bluff was cracked open by the mouth of a canyon and it was obvious that this was the point to which the tracks were leading them.

So he quickened the pace, gauging the strength of his horse, riding in an arrow-straight line across the rolling wasteland towards the canyon. The greyness of the sky deepened into an ominous black. The wind borne rain drops became larger and heavier. Far to the north they could see the thunderhead, turned to molten yellow by each lightning flash. But the claps were just a faint, inoffensive rumbling.

The storm centre stayed clear of them but its widening band of wind and rain steadily enclosed them in a tightening circle of reduced visability that soon took the canyon mouth out of sight. They rode in single file, hunched ineffectually against the lashing weather that by turns pressed their sodden clothes against their bodies then billowed them out.

'I haven't seen any tracks for a mile!' John shouted above the roar of the wind and hiss of the rain.

'First rain since the wagons went through,' Edge yelled over his shoulder. 'It's washing out the sign.'

'Then how do you know where you're going?' Elizabeth shouted from the rear of the line.

'Instinct, ma'am!' Edge called in reply. 'Kind of like female intuition, but more reliable.'

It was not a satisfactory answer, but the brother and sister accepted Edge's cold tone and unhesitant progress as a token of the man's confidence in himself. There was also the fact, of which both were anxiously aware, that without the impassive stranger they were undoubtedly lost. With him – it remained to be seen.

Although Edge knew that a storm – particular a freak winter thunderstorm – could zig-zag across open country with perplexing speed, he maintained a course that kept the thunder and lightning on his right. But there was no way to judge the distance and when the trio came up against the towering, sheer face of the bluff he could not decide whether they were to the north or south of the canyon. He dismounted and lead his horse into a cleft in the rock. There was no room for the others and they watched him with dispirited resentment as he dug out the makings and wiped his hands in his pockets before rolling a cigarette. A match flared in the shelter of the natural windbreak.

'Why are we waiting here, for goodness sake?' the woman demanded, angrily unpeeling some strands of hair plastered to her cheek.

Edge blew smoke at her, but it was whipped away by the wind. 'Used up all my instinct, ma'am,' he replied. 'Now, I figure the train was heading for a canyon that cuts into this bluff –'

'Canyon?' John asked sharply, and exchanged a meaningful glance with his sister.

Edge nodded and fixed the man with a steady stare. 'Mean something to you?'

'We're looking for a canyon. It's where Elizabeth and I have to go before we continue on to Summer.'

Edge spat out a leaf of tobacco. 'This country's full of them, feller. But one particular one is either north or south of here. Now we can either toss a coin and all ride together, or we can split up and check out both ways at once.'

Elizabeth was sitting high in the saddle, her head cocked to one side as if listening for something. The sadness in her eyes seemed to indicate she had little hope of picking up anything. But then she nodded her head emphatically. 'It's the one, John.'

Her brother eyed her without conviction. 'How can you possibly know, Liz?' he asked.

'I just do.'

Edge flicked his cigarette out into the wind and watched it driven away. 'Female intuition?' he suggested wryly.

'Something like that,' the woman defended.

30

'Does the little voice happen to point out which way we should go to find the place?'

She pointed a finger to the north. 'That way. And not far.'

Edge sighed, led his horse out from the shelter of rock and mounted. 'I got nothing to lose but time and ten thousand dollars,' he murmured.

'Liz could be right, Mr Edge,' John said. 'She and Byron were very close.'

'I'm a Walt Whitman fan but I don't commune with him,' Edge said wryly. 'Maybe that's because he's still alive?'

He nodded for Elizabeth to lead the way, but she held back to show him a hate filled glare.

'Byron Day,' she flung at him. 'He was our brother until he was murdered.'

She spurred her horse forward and John fell in behind her, giving Edge a quizzical glance as he passed. Edge trailed at the rear, still wearing the expression of melancholy despondency that pulled his cruel features into such an incongruous pattern and which had aroused John's curiosity. But if the ugly young man thought Edge was suffering contrition because of his flippancy, he was wrong. For the half-breed's sadness had come from out of the past, the woman's announcement recalling another dead brother. A teenager named Jamie whose agonising death had thrust Edge into a life as barren and dangerous as the Badlands through which they were riding.*

Edge was jerked back into the present by a sound that burst through the noise of the downpour and was much more ominous than that of wind and rain. John and Elizabeth Day heard it at the same time and reined their horses to a halt. Terror took hold of their features and then exerted a vice-like grip as they stared at each other – then at Edge.

'Yeah, you've got it,' Edge murmured as the syncopated beat of a water drum rose to its maximum pitch and held it. 'Seems like some Sioux ghost cut in on Byron's line and fed the lady a bum steer.'

'Perhaps they're friendly?' Elizabeth suggested nervously,

*See: Edge – The Loner.

forcing herself not to look along the bluff in the direction from which the drumbeat was coming.

'Only one way to find out,' Edge said easily, wheeling his horse into a shuffling turn. 'But it means getting close to them. I'm for racial harmony but that don't sound like my song they're playing.'

The Days began to wheel their horses.

'*No! Please!*' The words were screamed at the top of a man's voice and punctuated by a high-pitched wail of mind-bending agony. The drumbeat finished abruptly and a dozen warcries split the rain-washed air.

'They ain't friendly,' Edge muttered sourly.

'He's an American!' Elizabeth gasped.

'So are they,' Edge answered as the drumming began again, masking another, weaker scream of pain. 'But the line goes back further. That's what it's all about.'

'We can't just go away,' Elizabeth insisted.

'We can do whatever the hell we want,' Edge told her. 'It's a free country – unless some of us get noble and try to join the party along the bluff.'

The woman's eyes poured scorn upon him, then she swung her gaze towards her brother and her expression became imploring. 'John?' she demanded.

He seemed about to ignore her plea, but a deep-throated groan sounded from out of the rain.

'For God's sake, just kill me!' the tortured man screamed.

John, still afraid, tried to conquer his fear by action. He jerked the Remington rifle from its boot and worked the bolt to feed a shell into the breech. 'You stay here,' he commanded his sister. 'I'll see what can be done.'

'You're going to let him go alone?' the woman demanded of Edge.

John held back, waiting for his response. His confidence in his decision, small at the outset, seemed to be chipped away by each beat on the drum.

Edge ran a hand across the prickly stubble on his jaw. 'Lady,' he said with a sigh. 'I'm not the kind of guy who has to go looking for trouble. My share just comes naturally of its own accord.'

The scorn in her green eyes expanded and she raised her shoulders and drew in a deep breath, as if to sigh. But then her lips parted and she emitted a piercing scream. The drumbeat was abruptly curtailed and in the sudden silence her brother stared at her in disbelief.

'Crazy lady,' Edge hissed as he slid from his horse. He hooked out an arm and lifted the woman clear of her saddle, thudding her to the ground.

John gave a grunt of surprise and swung the rifle around to cover Edge. But he stayed his finger on the point of squeezing the trigger. The half-breed had taken the reins of his own horse and that of Elizabeth and pressed them into her trembling hand. He fixed her with a glittering, ice-cold stare from between narrowed lids.

'Hold them,' he snarled. 'And if anyone but me or the white knight here gets close, shoot yourself.' He glared up at the white-faced John. 'Get off the charger, feller,' he ordered. 'This ain't cavalry weather.'

John did as he was told, and thrust the reins of his horse towards his sister. She tried to speak, but the awesome realisation of what she had done took a constricting grip on her throat.

'Forget it,' Edge rasped at her, drawing his revolver. 'Stay quiet or the next sound you make could be your last.'

'My goodness,' she managed to gasp as she pulled the pepperbox from her jacket pocket and crouched down between the nervous horses and the cliff face.

It had only been a few moments since the woman's scream had silenced the drumbeat but now, as Edge raised a finger to his slightly parted lips and beckoned for Day to fall in beside him, it seemed as if an eternity had passed without the ominous thud of fist upon taut skin.

The two men moved along the foot of the sheer rock wall, shoulder-to-shoulder, eyes narrowed against the wind-driven rain as they raked the ground ahead. Rifle and revolver muzzles swung to left and right.

Four braves, spread out in line abreast, materialised across the path of the white men. Surprise held them in check for a split second. They were Teton Dakotas, stocky, brown-faced braves dressed in quill ornamented buckskin pants and a variety of stolen jackets. A few sodden eagle feathers decorated their headbands which failed to keep the long, greased hair from blowing across their faces. They wore no paint. Each carried a Winchester rifle.

'Savages!' Day spat out and blasted a hole in the chest of the brave on one end of the line.

Edge dived to the ground as three Winchesters roared to echo the report of the Remington. Day went into a crouch as bullets whined off into the rain. With cool precision, Edge emptied the single-action revolver at the Indians as they fumbled with the levers. He took aim across a crooked forearm, sending a shell burrowing into the stomach of each brave. As the slick blood pumped from the wounds and the braves folded forward, clutching themselves and dropping their rifles, he swung the revolver back along the line. Three skulls cracked and ejected red-stained fragments of brain matter under the impact of the heavy calibre bullets.

Edge glanced at Day and saw he was struggling with the bolt of his jammed rifle. 'Leave it,' he snapped, getting on to all fours and scampering across to the sprawled bodies. He snatched up two Winchesters and tossed one of them towards Day. 'This is no time for brand loyalty.'

He hurled his revolver against the cliff and went full-length to the ground as a volley of rifle fire sounded and bullets tore into the cooling flesh of the dead Indians. Day discarded his own rifle for the Winchester and gave a gasp of horror as he felt the tacky wetness of Teton Sioux blood on the stock. But as a shower of rock splinters stung his face from another fusillade of shots the revulsion exploded into anger. He glared through the teeming, billowing curtain of rain towards the gun flashes and swung the rifle barrel to left and right, spraying the area with a deadly hail of fire.

He was rewarded with the sound of three screams. But four more braves came forward at a run, their faces contorted by blood lust as their mouths hung wide in deep-throated warcries. They saw Day and angled in towards him, two with rifles and two with revolvers. They were unaware of Edge, flat on the ground amongst their dead, until his first shot splatted through the throat of one of them and burst out through the top of the brave's head.

They faltered, torn between two targets. A brave with a revolver took a bullet in the groin from Day's rifle and fell sideways with a scream. Another brave tripped over him and pitched towards Edge. The half-breed, his face seemingly frozen into a smile of evil enjoyment, raised his rifle. The brave tried to avert his head but failed. The Winchester muzzle smashed into his snarling teeth and then belched a bullet. His entire head seemed to shatter into a million tiny fragments.

As one brave sheered to the side to become lost behind the rain, another fired at Day, the bullet jerking the man's fur hat from his head. Day's aim was lower and his bullet gouged into the Indian's right eye. The brave injured in the groin writhed on the ground, his clothing dark with the watered-down blood of his brothers. Day took aim at him.

'Save it,' Edge muttered, getting to his feet and moving over to look at the man's agony. The brave attempted to roll away from Edge, but the half-breed drew back his foot and swung it forward. The toe of his boot made contact with the Indian's chin, forcing back his head and breaking his neck with a sharp crack.

Day let out his pent up breath in a long sigh. 'You looked like you enjoyed doing that, Edge,' he accused.

Edge crouched down, glanced around him for a sign of a new attack, then began to empty the spare Winchesters of their loads. He nodded for Day to do the same and showed his teeth in a cold grin. 'Maybe you like riding the plains,' he muttered.

'What?' Day asked as he pushed shells into his pockets.

'I get a kick out of Sioux,' Edge answered wryly, and sprang upright as gunfire sounded.

Six small calibre shots rang out in quick succession. The sound came from the general direction of where the woman had been told to wait.

'Liz!' Day shouted frantically and sprang forward into a run. Edge went after him, both men sending up splashes of water as their pounding feet plunged into muddied pools.

Elizabeth was standing out in the open, one hand clutching the reins of the horses. In the other was the still smoking pepperbox. The Indian who had run out on his fellow braves was slumped on the ground at her feet. His face was towards the low clouds and rain spattered into the gaping red hole where once he had had a nose. His mouth hung open as if in surprise.

'My goodness!' the woman exclaimed, and swallowed the nausea that rose in her throat. 'I think I killed him.'

'He sure won't smell good any more,' Edge muttered, and fired from the hip.

A young buck, stooped almost double as he crept up on the woman from the side, pitched forward with a bullet in his heart. The waterdrum slung around his neck on twine burst beneath the weight of his body. Escaping water flushed his blood away from his unmoving body.

'Ten's a nice round number,' Edge muttered and searched the face of the woman with his hooded eyes. 'For you? Or do you want to try another scream, ma'am?'

Elizabeth tried to match the intensity of his gaze, but suddenly the slight colour left in her cheeks drained away and her eyes swivelled up in their sockets. She made a small, gurgling sound and collapsed into a heap. Her brother tried to catch her and missed. Edge made a grab for the reins and caught two sets. His own horse reared and galloped off into the rain.

'If she's died of fright it'll save us tossing for who rides two up,' Edge muttered, starting to lead the horses along the foot of the cliff.

CHAPTER FOUR

THE Tetons' ponies were tethered at the mouth of the canyon. They eyed Edge nervously as he approached, leading the Days' mounts. He unfastened the tethers, sighted across the animals' backs and fired a shot. The ponies bolted into the freedom of the storm-lashed Badlands, their unshod hooves quickly taking them out of earshot. Edge whirled at the approach of running footfalls but lowered the Winchester as Day lumbered into sight, the unconscious Elizabeth in his arms.

'Scattered their ponies,' Edge said, tethering the horses.

Relief flooded Day's face, to be immediately wiped away as a low groan came from deeper within the canyon's mouth. 'I'd forgotten!' he said, aghast.

'Must have been all the excitement,' Edge said sourly, moving towards the source of the sound.

'Oh, dear God,' Day gasped and hurriedly lowered his sister to the ground, as if he feared his own strength would drain away and he might drop her.

The man who was no longer a man, was naked. They had cut off his genitals, but this only as the climax of their torture schedule. First he had been scalped. Then a score of cuts had been carved into his flesh so that his body was a mass of dangling flaps of sliced skin. The rain had not yet washed away all the white crystals of rock salt which had been poured into the open wounds. He was hanging upside down from a framework of lances lashed together by rope: held in place by twine which had cut through his ankles to the bone.

Day vomited and as his sister groaned and shook her head, he threw himself in front of her, hiding the horribly mutilated figure from her.

Incredibly, the victim of the Teton's torture still clung to a tenuous thread of life. He sensed the newcomers and his eyes opened. But they were glazed by his agony and he could not see them. A moan bubbled in his throat and he tried to lift his free hanging arms to ward off fresh viciousness.

'Relax, feller,' Edge told him easily. 'It's over for you.'

'Kill him!' Day rasped, clasping his sister around her shoulders and hugging her to him.

Edge eyed the man's suffering with an impassive expression. He had seen too much of broken bodies; witnessed more blood-letting than the human mind could take; been present on countless occasions when man's inhumanity to man was taken to the extremes of agony. He could have been driven into the realms of insanity by his experiences: or he could become a heartless machine fashioned into the form of a man. Edge was not mad and therefore he was nothing more than an animal drained of every ounce of compassion. But not of memory. He looked at the pathetic struggles of the helpless victim and recalled another occasion when he saw the results of barbaric Indian torture. It had been a different tribe, using different techniques, but it all came out the same in the end – agonising, lingering death.*

'It's his life,' Edge said coldly. 'What there is left of it. He has to say.'

The man's lips moved and Edge stooped down to put his ear close to his face. 'I'll tell . . . you . . . something . . . If you'll end it.'

His breath smelled bad and something moist – perhaps blood – bubbled in his throat as he forced out each word.

'Go to . . . Summer,' the man rattled when Edge nodded. 'Out to the rivers . . . the rivers.' The moisture flooded over his lips and ran into his nostrils. One of the knives had cut deep. It was blood. 'Haven,' he managed with his dying breath.

'Kill him, for mercy's sake!' Day screamed.

'Can't kill a dead man,' Edge said, straightening up. With a casualness that belied his usual agility at drawing the weapon, the half-breed reached up behind his neck and slid an open razor from the leather pouch he wore under his shirt. He sliced through both lengths of twine with a single slashing motion. The bloodied body slumped heavily to the ground. He replaced the razor and turned to look out of the canyon.

Within its protective walls the rain fell almost lightly, lacking the power of the north wind. But now, almost as if it had spent its last reserves of forceful energy as a contribution to the violence of men, the storm was blowing itself out across the wasteland. Overhead, the blackness of the low

*See: Edge – Apache Death.

clouds was giving way to a lighter coloration.

'Let's move,' Edge told the Days as the woman got to her feet, saw the dead man and spun away.

'No!' she said sharply, as if steeling herself against a further reaction to sudden death. Then she continued: 'This is the place. The canyon where John and I had to come.'

'You came, you saw and you conquered everything it had,' Edge told her. 'But one band of Sioux gunning for whites could mean the whole damn nation is trying for the final solution.' He prodded the corpse with the rifle barrel. 'There has to be a better way to die than that.'

'It won't take long,' John Day insisted, crossing to where the horses were tethered and delving a hand into the centre of the bedroll strapped to his animal.

He brought out something wrapped in sacking, forming a package about the size of a shoebox. As he moved away, heading further into the canyon, Elizabeth fell in behind him. They angled towards the side and halted before a natural alcove worn into the sheer rock.

'You're certain this is the one?' John asked.

Elizabeth nodded. 'I know, John. I've never been more certain of anything in my life before.'

'Is this a good place, do you think?' he asked her, pointing into the alcove.

'I think so, John.'

He untied the string holding the sacking in place and carefully removed the protective material. Edge moved to one side so that he could look between the brother and sister and see what was happening. John was holding a plain cross which in the dull light of the slackening storm had the dull sheen of gold. The upright member of the ornament was set into a flat base so that the cross stood solidly when John set it on the flat rock which formed the floor of the alcove. The couple stood with heads bent for several moments, in attitudes of private prayer. John finished first, then Elizabeth, and they turned away from the shrine.

Edge was in the process of mounting the woman's horse

but neither of them took exception to the act.

'It has an inscription,' Elizabeth told him. '"In memory of Byron Day who died close by in the service of his country",' she quoted.

'Nice gesture,' Edge said easily. 'It'll be appreciated by the first saddletramp or Sioux brave who wanders by here. Ain't much that melts down easier than gold.'

'That's what I told her,' John said. 'But she wanted to do it. She's a rather headstrong woman.'

'I've noticed,' Edge muttered.

'There isn't a grave,' Elizabeth said sadly. 'Not for any of the soldiers who died here. By the time the Colonel reached Summer and they sent men out here, there were only the skeletons left. Coyotes and buzzards, the army told us.'

'It happened last August,' Day put in.

'It's a wicked month,' Edge answered. 'Now, do you want to sing hymns or burn incense – or can we move out to where the greenbacks grow?'

Day swung up into his saddle and held out a hand for his sister.

'What about him?' the woman asked, pointing towards the dead man without looking at him. 'Shouldn't we bury him?'

Edge spat through the rain, which had been reduced to a lazy drizzle. 'Does he look as if he cares, one way or the other?'

'My goodness, that's hardly the point,' she flung at him. 'A man who died so savagely deserves a decent burial.'

'Leave him where he is,' her brother urged. 'This isn't Philadelphia, Liz. Nature takes care of these things out here. As we have good reason to know.'

She seemed about to argue her case, then shrugged, took hold of her brother's hand and hauled herself up behind him. Edge led the way out of the canyon and waited for John to point the way to Summer. He nodded his head towards the south.

The wind had died away completely now and the rain clouds were breaking up immediately overhead, where the noon sun was suffusing the sky with a faint tinge of yellow.

They had to steer their horses among the bodies of the ten Indians, sprawled along the foot of the bluff in attitudes of violent death.

'My goodness, did we kill all those?' Elizabeth exclaimed in awe.

John screwed his neck around to smile at her. 'We did very well, Liz,' he said, reining in his horse to dismount and retrieve his fur hat, now with a hole drilled through it.

'There's a lot more where they came from,' Edge said as John climbed back into the saddle.

'What do you mean?' Elizabeth asked, glancing anxiously across the vastness of the Badlands, unveiled again by the brightening weather of the afternoon.

'Indians,' Edge tossed over his shoulder. 'Neither you nor your brother should get too high and mighty about blasting a few. All kinds, in all kinds of tribes. So you kill a few Sioux? It's still a big tribe – one of the strongest ones in the country.'

'So what?' the woman demanded, anxious to preserve her post-shock pride in helping to kill the savages.

Edge shrugged. 'I just figure it'll take more than two Days to make that one weak,' he muttered.

CHAPTER FIVE

THEY passed the town marker for Summer – *Warmest Hearted Town in Northlands* – just after sundown. They had covered the more than fifty miles of barren country from the canyon in two gruelling stages, separated by a short rest for coffee and beans which exhausted the Days' supplies.

The town was at the dead end of nowhere, built in a hollow formed by three hills with the south side bounded by the Old Creek tributary of the Cheyenne River. The marker

41

was sited on the southern bank of the creek which was spanned by a trestle bridge.

Elizabeth shrieked and tightened her arms around John's waist as the boards creaked and swayed under the horses' hoofs. The clatter of their progress covered the sound of her fear and the noise of the town. But as Day and Edge reined their mounts to a walk between the neat one and two storey frame houses flanking the main street they heard the jangling notes of an out-of-tune piano and the voice of a woman singing against the raucous barrage of drunken shouting.

The noise was coming from an area ablaze with lights about two hundred yards down the street. And the noisy brightness of what lay ahead seemed to be magnified by the subdued peace of this end of town. To left and right of the newcomers as they moved along the rutted dirt street the houses sat in brooding silence behind well-tended gardens bounded by white picket fences. Only meagre cracks of light under doors and between shutters on the windows betrayed the presence of occupants.

They crossed an intersection with neatly painted signs which told them they were on August Street at July. There were more houses, less well tended, on the cross street. August became brighter with business premises that did not put up the shutters when night threw its shadows over the town.

'Evening, folks,' a gangling man in his sixties called from the doorway of Frank's Livery. 'Welcome to Summer.' He grinned and blew on his hands. 'Don't feel like it sounds, does it?'

'Looks like there's a hot time happening down the street,' Edge answered, angling his mount across to the livery entrance.

The man broadened his grin and glanced down towards the source of the noise and light. 'Sure is a lot of folks on Solar Circle with money to burn, mister,' he said as Edge slid from the saddle. 'But the only one really getting any warmth out of it is Millie Pitt. Guess you're heading for The Gates of Heaven, uh?'

'Ain't we all?' Edge said, handing the reins of his horse to the man.

He laughed. 'Sure is the truth. But I'm talking about Millie Pitt's hotel. That's what she calls it. 'Course, local folk reckon as how it ought to say Steps into Hell over the door. Ten dollars a day, mister.'

'Pretty high, even for paradise,' Edge said.

The man had stopped grinning when he mentioned the rate. Now his gaunt features took on a hard expression, as if he expected trouble and was confident he could handle it. 'I'm talking about feed, water and a stall for your horse. What the Pitt charges for human animals is her business.'

Edge shrugged, surprising the man, and turned away, sliding the Winchester from the saddle boot. 'Ain't my horse,' he said. 'I just borrowed it.'

'My goodness, that's an exorbitant price,' Elizabeth Day said shrilly. 'Come on, John, we'll find another place.'

Edge was already ambling down the street towards Solar Circle and the woman snatched the reins of her horse from the man then made to follow the half-breed.

'Ain't another place in town,' the man said easily. 'And you leave a couple of fine animals like that unattended in Summer, they'll get stole soon as you turn your back.'

'Warmest hearted town!' Elizabeth exclaimed angrily.

'Sure enough is,' the man replied, rekindling his grin. 'Course, since Haven set himself up in the Bridal Suite at The Gates of Heaven and the new people started to come to town, things got changed some. You got to pay a little more for everything nowadays, ma'am. Law of supply and demand. Good horses are in short supply. And so are stalls to keep them in.' His expression hardened again and his eyes became greedy as they stared at the woman, then swung to her brother. 'One day in advance. That'll be twenty dollars for the two animals.'

John dug inside his jacket for money.

'You better take good care of them,' the woman warned.

'Animal gets stole, you get your money back,' the man answered, watching John's actions as he counted four fives

43

off his roll. 'Only I ain't never lost an animal yet.' He took the money and pushed it into his boot then reached into the doorway behind him and brought out a Spencer repeater. 'Either me or my partner's on guard twenty-four hours a day, folks. Your animals will be safer than you are in this town.'

John Day unstrapped the two bedrolls and slid out the Winchester before standing back to allow the man to take the horses.

'I suppose there's no other place in town except for this Pitt woman's hotel for us to stay?' Elizabeth asked sullenly.

'All we needed was just the one hotel before Mr Haven came,' the man replied. 'Just didn't get the passing trade. And there ain't been no time to build another since the money rush started.'

'Come on, John,' Elizabeth urged.

The man nodded. 'You'd better hurry and catch up with your friend. He looks the kind of feller who can handle trouble. And in Summer that's the only thing we ain't got a shortage of.'

'What am I?' Day demanded. 'A handful of chopped liver.'

The man shrugged. 'Just thought I'd mention it. A friendly warning, like.'

'He's no friend of ours,' Elizabeth shot back, and caught hold of her brother's arm to start down the street. 'And we can take care of ourselves, anyway.'

The man shook his head to their backs, then led the two horses into the livery stable, contemplating his chances o₁ inheriting the animals on the grounds that possession was nine points of the law.

Down August Street, where it was intersected by September to form Solar Circle, Edge glanced at the elaborately decorated façade of The Gates of Heaven Hotel. It was a three storey building on a prime corner lot. Lights blazed brightly from the first floor windows and spilled out from the four sets of batswing doors, as if trying to escape from the raucous din of the saloon. The kerosene burned on lower wicks in the hotel rooms above, shining out on to railed balconies which were hung with painted wooden cut-outs of winged angels. Flanking each set of doors were a pair of more ornate guardians of paradise, carved into three-dimensional models with their arms outstretched in welcome.

'What do you want here, mister?' a man asked.

Edge turned to look at him. He was a big man with long legs, broad shoulders and a stomach that seemed to start beneath the lowest of his many chins and reached a wide girth around his waist before being pinched in by his double-holstered gunbelt. He was holding open his ankle-length coat to exhibit the pair of Navy Colts in the holsters and a tin star pinned to his black shirt. His face was as fleshy as the rest of him and his eyes seemed to be glittering from the bottom of deep valleys of fat. They met Edge's hard stare of inquiry and held fast.

'Who's asking?'

'Sheriff Truman. He stills wants to know.'

'Curiosity's killed a lot of cats, sheriff,' Edge answered easily.

'Jesus, another one of them,' the lawman rasped. 'I figured you for one and I was right. Guess I don't have to ask. You came to see Haven.'

'Law against it?'

Truman pushed something out of his teeth with his tongue and spat it at the wall of the church which occupied this corner of the inter-section. 'There ought to be, but there ain't,' he answered. 'But we got all the other laws you've heard about, mister. Don't break any of them and there won't be any need for me to talk to you again.'

He closed his coat and buttoned it against the night cold. With no guns or a star showing, he was just a fat man with small, untrusting eyes.

'One what, sheriff?' Edge asked, looking again at the hotel, then at The Last Rose restaurant on an opposite corner which was also doing good business. The final corner of the intersection was taken up by the Summer County Bank. It wasn't open but lights burned inside, and two men could be seen sitting at a table, playing cards. They could use only one half of the table. Their rifles rested across the other section.

'Bounty hunter,' Truman answered sourly. 'I been the law in Summer for twenty years. In all that time only strangers to pass through were on the Deadwood bound stage. Decent people on legal business. Why, the Ball brothers and their side-kicks never come within twenty miles of town. Now, because of them hitting the army train and that crazy Haven wanting their blood, we've filled to overflowing with the riff-raff of the territory.' He sighed. 'Guess one more won't make much difference.'

Edge had his back towards the sheriff. It was impossible to see through the misted up windows of the saloon, but he could get a view over the top of a pair of batswings to where a blonde-headed woman in a low-cut dress was leaning across a piano and singing a song which was lost amid the shouts and cheers of her drunken audience. 'You got a law about not hitting a man who runs off at the mouth?' he asked.

Truman knew what the half-breed was talking about and started to unbutton his coat. The fastenings were fixed so that all he had to do was insert his finger under the lowest button and run it upwards. He had only reached the crest of his bulbous stomach when Edge gave a backwards flick of his wrist and the stock of the Winchester smashed up into the lawman's crotch. The breath whooshed out between his clenched teeth as his legs buckled and he fell heavily to his knees, his pudgy hands clasped over his groin.

'Bastard!' Truman flung at Edge as the half-breed turned to face him.

'I ain't that either,' Edge said softly and brought up his knee hard into the kneeling man's face.

Truman was flung backwards and his head crashed heavily against the church door. He crumpled into an un-conscious heap in the porch as the door was swung inwards. The priest stared down in astonishment at the still form, then turned his wide eyes towards Edge.

'It's okay,' the half-breed said. 'He knocked on your door by mistake. It was the second one he made.'

'What happened?' Elizabeth Day asked as she and John halted in front of the church and saw the slumped form of the sheriff.

She posed the question to the priest, who was a tall, narrow-faced man in his mid-thirties. He had thinning sandy hair and skin pocked by the scars of smallpox. He recovered from his shock and crouched down beside the unconscious man.

'He wasn't polite,' Edge said.

'It's Sheriff Truman,' the priest exclaimed. 'You hit him?'

Edge took out the makings and rested the Winchester against his leg as he rolled a cigarette. 'Once for riff-raff and once for bastard. If he thinks of any new words when he wakes up, I'll be over at the hotel. It looks like its closer to my idea of heaven than what you've got inside, father.'

He struck a match on the porch wall and fired his cigarette before turning and going across the intersection towards the hotel.

'The hotel's full,' the priest called after him, using a handkerchief to wipe blood from the sheriff's split lip. 'But I think Bob Truman will accommodate you in one of his cells.'

It had been a bad day for Edge. First he had been almost scalded by boiling coffee, then shot at, railroaded into a fight he wanted no part of and finally insulted by a hick town lawman. That added up to a lot of anger in a man such as he and lamming into the sheriff had been a calculated act which did nothing to relieve his feelings. It was therefore fortunate for the priest that his taunt was lost against the waves of noise flooding from the saloon.

So, as the Days stooped to help the priest lift and carry Truman into the church, Edge entered The Gates of Heaven with a full load of contained frustration still waiting to be unleashed. He stood in the doorway for long moments, his hooded eyes raking the crowded, smoke-filled room, the cigarette angling from one corner of his thin-lipped mouth. There were two bar counters taking the form of quarter circles in the far corners of the big room. Across the rear

47

wall, running between the bars and as high as they were, was a stage and it was on this that the melancholic-faced pianist and the big-breasted, over-painted singer were finishing their part of the saloon's entertainment programme.

They had the noisy attention of about half the patrons. The rest were engaged in the games of chance set out on a dozen tables spread across the front area of the saloon. But as the singer reached the end of her song and her accompaniest struck up an off-key introductory piece, even some of the gamblers turned their attention towards the stage. They added their roars of approval to the cheers of the men clustered in front of the stage and at the bars as a dozen long-legged chorus girls in cut-away gowns high-kicked their way into view.

Edge eyed the flashing legs and swaying bodies appreciatively for a few moments then returned his attention to the audience. Apart from a score or so of house girls, the patrons of the saloon comprises upwards of fifty men. Maybe half of these were farmers and ranchers come in from the surrounding country, or local citizens. But the remainder were the riff-raff of whom the sheriff had spoken. They were easy to pick out, no matter whether they were attired in eastern suits and had recently washed up and shaved or if they had come in straight from the trail with dust still clinging to their stubbled jaws and western threads. For they were the watchful ones, never able to completely relax, always flicking anxious glances around them, constantly reappraising their surroundings as they went through the motions of leering at exposed female flesh or willing the dice to roll the right combination.

'Like what you see, stranger?' a woman asked.

Because Edge was just the kind of man he had been pinpointing in the saloon, he was aware of the woman's approach. He had seen her, on the periphery of his sweeping glances across the saloon, come out from behind a desk set at an angle at the foot of the stairway which canted gently up one wall of the room. He had noted the forced elegance of the way she carried her statuesque body and recognised the avariciousness that gleamed in her beautiful eyes. The eyes, large, blue and clear, were all she had retained of her youthful good looks. Now, as Edge turned to look at her he saw the extent to which the passing years had robbed the woman of what had once been a proud beauty. Paint could not entirely conceal the ravaging lines on her face; grey roots sprang up in her red dyed hair and constricting whalebone showed as ridges beneath her bright green dress. She was almost fifty and trying to look twenty. His cool eyes examined her from head to toe, offering no clue to what he was thinking.

'You Millie Pitt?' he asked.

She showed well-made, very expensive dentures in a smile that was supposed to be beguiling. 'The one they call the Pitt,' she replied. 'Because I'm so deep no man's ever got to the bottom of me.'

'I prefer my tail younger so I won't even try, ma'am,' Edge said. 'Where will I find George Haven?'

The Pitt had been in her business a long time and had learned to take insults, spoken or implied, without losing her surface coolness. 'Figured you might want to see the Colonel,' she said easily. 'These days men come to The Gates of Heaven for one of three things – drinking, whoring or to see Haven. Men being men, I get my share of the action – sooner or later. Haven has the Bridal Suite. Third floor at the back. It's quiet.'

Edge nodded. 'Obliged.'

'Edge!' a man yelled as the half-breed made his way towards the foot of the stairway.

He heard his name above the noise from the other end of the big room. He halted and started to turn. A handgun went off and an eerie silence intruded into the saloon. The men stopped yelling their approval of the dancing girls, the girls finished their act abruptly and the piano player halted in the middle of a bar. The quietness took up to three seconds to become complete and lasted another two as every eye in the place swivelled to the doorway, saw Sherriff Truman standing there, and travelled to where Millie Pitt stood. Everybody except the lawman ignored Edge.

'I told you, Bob,' the madam spoke into the silence.

'Anybody fires a gun in my place has to answer to me.'

The woman's expression was as ice cold as her tone. But a burning anger was raging just beneath the surface, ready to explode out into the open at the slightest provocation.

Truman's anger was visible in every trembling ounce of his obese frame. He was standing in the doorway with the batswing doors resting against his back. One of the Navy Colts was coming up from where he had fired it into the floor. Dried blood stained his series of chins.

'You're under arrest, Edge,' the lawman rasped, levelling the Colt, ignoring the woman.

Edge was standing sideways on to the sheriff, the Winchester held low down in both hands and aimed at Truman. His finger was curled around the trigger. 'Third mistake tonight, feller,' he said easily. 'Wasting a bullet into the floor like that.'

'It goes for you, too, mister,' Millie Pitt hissed at Edge. 'No shooting in my place.'

Now it was Edge who became the centre of attention. He didn't have to look around the room to know that every eye in the place was focused upon him. A sixth sense born of living in the shadow of sudden death for so long told him all he needed to know.

'People have tried to throw me out of better places than this, ma'am,' he drawled, keeping his hooded eyes fastened upon Truman.

'You're goin' to get carried out of his one,' Truman said sharply and squeezed the trigger.

Edge dropped into a crouch and fired the Winchester. Truman's bullet whistled over his head and thudded into the stairway bannister. The sheriff yelled and went sideways, his revolver spinning away from his numbed fingers. A streak of blood appeared on the back of his hand where Edge's bullet ploughed a meaty furrow from the middle finger joint to the wrist.

A ripple of awed surprise trickled through the crowd of watchers. Truman doubled over, pressing his injured hand to his middle and trying to staunch the flow of blood with the other one. Edge moved towards him, his gait casual but his expression purposeful.

'You heard what the Pitt said,' he told the lawman.

'I said I handle my own trouble, mister!' the madam snarled.

Edge ignored her and prodded Truman with the muzzle of the Winchester. 'Get up and get out,' he said softly.

'My gun?' Truman croaked, nodding towards his Colt on the floor.

Edge stooped and picked up the revolver. He slid it into his own empty holster. 'Obliged,' he said. 'Mighty generous the way you Dakotas lawmen donate your spare guns to the needy.'

Truman eyed him with confusion through his pain. 'What's that supposed to mean?' he croaked.

Edge jerked the Winchester towards the doors. 'Another story, sheriff,' he said. 'For another time, maybe*. Right now you'd better go see the sawbones about that wound. This rifle belonged to a Sioux buck. No telling what he painted on the shells before he loaded up.'

'You run into Indians on your way here?' Truman asked, suddenly forgetting his pain.

A lot of other people in the saloon were abruptly more interested in Edge's news than in the possibility of further violence.

Edge nodded, and narrowed his eyes as he saw John and Elizabeth Day enter the saloon and pull up short. 'Coyotes should be having them for supper right about now,' he answered.

He saw the woman shudder.

'I better check my deputies,' Truman said, suddenly straightening and whirling towards the door.

Edge glanced quickly around the room, paying particular heed to the men with the anxious eyes. 'We only made ten Indians into the good kind,' he said as he headed for the foot of the stairway.

A small, wiry man in an eastern suit stepped out into Edge's path. 'You saying there's more Sioux stirred up out

*See: *Edge – Seven Out of Hell*.

there in the Badlands?' he asked softly.

The half-breed surveyed him through hooded eyes. 'Scare you?'

'Should it?' the man answered, as impassive as Edge.

'Not if you stay in Summer,' Edge told him easily. 'Sheriff'll protect you.'

'That barrel of lard!' the Pitt put in sourly as Edge waved his hand at the small man, who moved to the side.

Edge started up the stairway. 'Figured Truman for a guy able to stop all the bucks,' he said with a shrug.

CHAPTER SIX

'YOU want to see me, sir?' the tall, dignified man at the head of the stairway demanded.

Haven was dressed in civilian garb of an immaculate white shirt with a black bootlace tie beneath an embroidered red vest worn above sharply creased striped pants and highly polished shoes. His head, crowned by a mane of iron grey hair, was held square and upright upon his shoulders by a metal collar around his neck upon which his clean-shaven jaw rested.

Edge eyed the man with cool reflection as, below in the saloon the Pitt yelled at her entertainers and dealers to restart giving the customers what they wanted. 'You look like you could be a Colonel,' he said.

'Ex-Colonel,' Haven corrected and rapped a thumb knuckle on the rigid collar. 'Invalided out of 5th United States Cavalry, sir.'

He returned Edge's open stare and the restriction of the collar allowed him to make only a slight nod of approval at what he saw.

'You also look rich,' Edge said. 'But I need to see proof

you're ten grand rich before I risk *my* neck looking for what you lost.'

'Come into my suite,' Haven rapped out, turning with what was almost a drill square gesture and leading the way along the carpeted corridor.

Double doors at the end gave on to an elegantly furnished sitting room. The furniture, carpeting, wall covering, pictures and bric-a-brac had set Millie Pitt back a lot of money. Edge guessed that Haven was doing a great deal towards helping her get a return on her investment. And he also decided that the most expensive item in the room was a petite girl of about eighteen with long black hair and big blue eyes who was lounging seductively on a sofa as she concentrated upon her time-consuming task of peeling black grapes. She was dressed in an almost sheer nightgown that clung tantilisingly to the voluptuous curves of her highly developed young body.

The girl ignored Edge as Haven crossed the room and sat down in an armchair set adjacent to the end of the sofa. In this position, the girl could insert prepared grapes into his mouth without any strain. And she was within easy reach of his smoothly manicured hands if the whim came over him.

'It's looking richer by the moment,' Edge said as he heeled the door closed behind him. 'But you're only showing me what money can buy.'

Haven chewed appreciatively on a grape then spat out the seed on to the carpet before sipping from a glass of champagne. 'You've created a good impression, young man,' he said in his throaty Boston-Irish accent. 'I like your style.' He accepted another grape, offered with high-priced, professional adoration. 'Yes indeed, Mr Edge . . . isn't it?'

'Truman's got a loud mouth,'

Haven nodded. 'I heard and I saw,' he said. 'That's a very tough bunch of men my reward offer brought into this town.'

Edge ambled over to a substantial looking Martha Washington chair and tested his weight on it. It didn't even groan. He rested the Winchester across the arms. 'All

53

kinds of men like that sort of money,' he said.

'Correct,' Haven answered. 'And a lot of them are prepared to go to extremes to get it. One such extreme would be to cut out the competition. That was an excellent tactic of yours – picking a fight with the sheriff. The way you won it showed every man in the saloon you aren't the kind of man to tangle with. An example is worth a thousand words of boasting.'

Edge dropped his cigarette on to the carpet and ground it out under his heel. The girl glared hatefully at him.

'Treat my guests as you would me, Cyn,' Haven said sharply and the words forced a smile to the girl's pretty face which she directed towards Edge. 'Cynthia gets paid for looking after the room as well as me,' Haven explained.

'Who's paying the boys downstairs?' Edge asked. 'They're living it up like every one of them's already collected the reward.'

'The money's still in the County Bank across the street,' Haven said with a note of irritation in his voice. 'You may have noticed the two Pinkerton men on guard in there. If you insist upon seeing the actual banknotes, I'll be happy to accompany you across and give authority for the safe to be opened.'

Edge pondered this a moment, then shook his head. 'I've met the Pitt and I've heard about the prices being charged in this town. You wouldn't be living here like a Roman emperor unless you could back your mouth with your money.'

Haven didn't like the choice of phrase, but betrayed it only with a tightening of his mouth line. 'Neither would I make a promise I could not keep to that band of cutthroats downstairs,' he said, and chewed on another grape.

'They don't seem over anxious to collect what you're offering,' Edge pointed out.

Haven shrugged and the movement seemed to cause him some pain. 'Most of them have a stake of sorts when they arrive and they are the sort who find it difficult to hold on to money. Millie Pitt is adept at helping them overcome their difficulties. And when they have sampled as many pleasures

54

of The Gates of Heaven as their money allows, they go out looking for what they came for.' He seemed about to shrug again, but recalled the discomfort and let it go at a sigh. 'They come and they go. Most of them are no-hopers. But every now and then, a man such as you stops by. It's what gives me continued faith that my property will be returned to me ultimately.'

Edge ran his fingers along the smooth barrel of the Winchester. 'You got faith in anybody else except me?' he asked.

'Cheroot, Cyn,' Haven said and the girl deftly plunged a hand into the neckline of her nightgown and withdrew what he wanted. He sniffed the cigar with great pleasure and then allowed the girl to light it. 'One man, very like you,' he said on a cloud of smoke. 'Businesslike, but not so extreme in his methods. Named Silas Hyman. Stayed in Summer only long enough to ask some questions then rode out for the canyon where my train was ambushed. I feel he might get a line to the Balls.'

Edge clicked his tongue against the roof of his mouth. 'About my age, inch or so shorter? Black hair and a mole on his chin?'

Haven was surprised. 'You know the man?' he asked, crinkling the wrinkled skin around his dark eyes.

'We've met,' Edge answered. 'He didn't get anywhere near the Balls. But he lost his own.'

The surprise became shock.. 'The Sioux you were talking about downstairs?' He shook his head. 'I figured that for a story to scare the competition into staying close to town.'

Edge spat on the carpet and watched the girl conceal her displeasure behind a wafer-thin smile. 'If it was a story, Silas Hyman sure got cut up by nothing,' he said. 'What am I looking for, Colonel?'

For the first time since Edge had met him, the half-breed saw the depth of Haven's feeling for his loss. A hate-filled rage rose to very near the surface of the man, who held it in check by the shortest of rein. 'Whatever is left of the contents of three wagonloads of personal effects,' he said with a catch in his voice. The girl reached out with another grape and he knocked her hand away with a vicious swipe. It hurt her but she bit back a cry of pain as she cowered on the sofa. 'Furniture imported from every corner of the world. Paintings by the Old Masters. Bone china. Crystal. Silverware. Clocks. Books.'

'Value?' Edge asked coldly, his tone in contrast to Haven's quivering voice.

'Probably priceless,' the Colonel replied immediately. 'But the reward money is based upon ten per cent of the total purchase price of the goods. Needless to say, I do not expect to recover the wine, brandy and cigars which were also on the train.'

Edge nodded. 'Maybe some of the other junk as well.'

'Junk!' Haven roared, then brought himself under control as he drew against his cheroot and glared at Edge. The half-breed was a cut above the other drifters which his reward offer had attracted. But only in terms of sly intelligence and the professional killer's instinct for self-preservation. One had only to look at him – unshaven, unwashed and unkempt – to see the stamp of the uncaring philistine on the man. He could not be expected to appreciate the finer things of life. 'There is no sliding scale for the reward,' he went on tightly. 'The full amount will be paid to the man who brings me what is left of my treasures – together with Thomas and Edward Ball and whichever of their gang of ruffians remain with them.' He leaned down stiffly to grind out his cheroot in the carpet pile. 'Dead of alive!'

Edge sniffed. 'Dead is easiest,' he said, and got to his feet.

'You sound as if you think the whole thing will be easy,' Haven replied. 'Do you have any idea where to look for the Balls?'

Edge eyed the girl who had recovered from her painful humiliation and was using her painted fingernails to peel more grapes. 'One I aim to keep to myself,' he said pointedly.

'You can speak in front of Cyn,' Haven assured him. 'I pay her well enough so that she doesn't need to make anything else by selling what she hears in this suite.'

'Nobody ever gets paid enough,' Edge said, and turned

towards the double doors just as they were flung wide, crashing back against the walls.

John and Elizabeth Day stood on the threshhold of the room, the man levelling his Winchester at Haven. The couple stared hatefully at the Colonel. Behind them, his pockmarked face wreathed with anxiety, stood the priest.

'What is the meaning of this intrusion?' Haven demanded angrily.

'Are you Colonel Haven?' John Day snapped.

'Please be reasonable!' the priest pleaded.

'He was responsible for Byron's death,' Elizabeth tossed over her shoulder and added fire to her hate as she stared again at the Colonel.

'That your personal business in Summer?' Edge asked easily, looking coolly at the girl. 'What you going to do after you shoot him – hang him out for the buzzards?'

'Stay out of this, Edge!' Day rasped. 'You know how personal it is.'

Haven was not the kind of man to be scared. For a soldier he had survived longer than the average by luck and judgement and he was prepared to meet death on its terms whenever it chose to strike. But the priest and the girl seemed to apportion his share of anxiety between them as the brother and sister advanced into the room.

'Byron Day,' Haven said evenly and raised a finger to inscribe an imaginery line on his forehead above his nose. 'Had a scar here.'

'You couldn't get volunteers to haul your crumby stuff from Fort Abercrombie to Fort Bridger,' Day snarled. 'So you just detailed Byron and the others. It wasn't army business. They were killed protecting your miserable home comforts.'

'Please?' the priest begged.

'They died following orders,' Haven said with a note of finality in his voice. 'Doing a soldier's duty.'

'Don't hand me that line of crap!' Day snarled, his hands trembling as they gripped the Winchester.

'You don't need it,' Edge put in. 'You're full of it already if you figure to blast Haven.'

57

'I told you to stay out!' Day yelled, not taking his glaring eyes away from the placid face of the Colonel.

'I'm already in,' Edge said. 'And with the pot stacked ten grand high I don't figure to fold. There are a few other guys downstairs who'll feel the same way. Kill the Colonel and every one of us will have ten thousand reasons to be sore at you.' He curled his lips back from his teeth and narrowed his eyes to mere glinting slits. 'And when I get sore, feller, it ain't me who feels the pain.'

It was a factor that neither of the Days had taken into consideration when planning their revenge. Now, both of them recognised the danger in the same instant. The girl on the sofa let out a soft sigh as she saw the anger drain from the brother and sister. The priest caught the expression and some of the stiffness went out of his tall frame.

'John!' Elizabeth said in awe and swung towards her brother.

He made a similar move towards her and her hand smacked against the rifle stock. John had relaxed his grip but suddenly tightened it to keep the Winchester from falling. His finger squezed the trigger.

The report was like a cannon in the confines of the room. The bullet riccochetted off Haven's rigid collar with a metallic clash and spun into Cyn's open mouth. She was no longer alive to utter a sound as she toppled from the sofa. Blood sprayed over her lips and spouted from the back of her head as the shell burst clear.

'Dear God!' Elizabeth gasped, gripping her brother's arm.

Day dropped the Winchester as if it had suddenly become red hot. The priest seemed undecided whether to advance into the room or turn tail and run back to his church in search of spiritual guidance. Haven fingered the bullet dent in his iron collar and reflected stoically upon his continued good luck. All of them stared down at the dead girl as her blood spread a widening stain across her nightgown, moulding the material tackily to her breasts.

'She didn't deserve to die like this,' the ex-soldier murmured.

'You only paid her money,' Edge said coldly. 'She was a whore. The big pay off had to come some time.'

Haven eyed him quizzically through his sadness.

'The wages of Cyn is death,' Edge said.

CHAPTER SEVEN

EVERY person in the room looked towards Edge with blatant distaste as running footfalls sounded on the stairway at the far end of the corridor.

'Doesn't death mean anything to you, for goodness sake?' Elizabeth asked hoarsely, clinging to her brother.

'I worry about my own,' he answered as the doorway became crowded with the curious.

The Pitt and the wiry framed man who had questioned Edge about the Sioux were at the front of the crush. The owner of The Gates of Heaven, noting that Edge was the only man in the room holding a gun, stared at him in deep hatred.

'I warned you once, mister!' she snarled. Then she saw the bloodied corpse and gave a shriek. 'You'll hang for this!' she screamed and spun around, to elbow her way back through the press of people.

The priest, recognising Edge as a lost cause, transferred his horrified gaze to Haven. 'I predicted this, Colonel,' he accused in the booming tone he normally reserved for fire and brimstone sermons. 'I warned that you would bring bloodshed to this town.'

'Go and tend your flock, padre,' Haven said softly. 'There's nothing you can do here.'

Most of those who had rushed up from the saloon now turned to go back down again, satisfied that it was not the man with the money who had been killed. Just a whore and there a lot more of those in The Gates of Heaven.

'Seems to me there's a black sheep in this part of the pasture he could work on,' the wiry man with the unwavering stare put in, still concentrating his attention on Edge.

He was now alone in the doorway and Edge examined him closely for the first time. Although he was no more than five feet six and probably carried less than a hundred and fifty pounds on his narrow frame, there was something about him to warn against discounting the man as an irritating nobody. Above his sparse body in its well-fitting, high-priced eastern suit, was a face with a kind of nondescript handsomeness. He had regular features that would merge easily into a crowd and be difficult to recall: unless he fixed the steady, open stare with his coal black eyes and backed it with a slightly crooked parting of his lips into a quarter smile. In this case, the object of his strangely searching humour would probably have difficulty in ever forgetting him. Edge, his eyes narrowed to slits, returned the frank examination, judging the man to be about his own age, from a vastly different background. But, apparent from the man's coolness in the presence of sudden death, Edge recognised the mark of past experiences which paralleled his own. Violent death, which could never be a friend to any man, was certainly no stranger to this one.

'Let's set the record straight before any wrong ideas start circulating,' Edge said softly. 'I've been the route of serving time for a murder I didn't commit.* Then it didn't matter too much. Right now I've got things to do. The avenging angels over there sent the dame to that big bordello in the sky.'

'It was an accident, for goodness sake,' Elizabeth protested as Edge waved his Winchester towards her and her brother.

'I will testify to that, my child,' the priest promised.

More footfalls sounded on the stairway as Haven suffered pain in giving a nod. 'Trooper Day would have made a good soldier, had he been given the time. I bear no grudge

*See: Edge – The Blue, The Grey And The Red.

60

against his kin for what they intended to do to me. The shooting was accidental.'

Millie Pitt, Sheriff Truman and a tall, thin man in a stovepipe hat and frock coat filed into the room. The madam, her over-painted face contorted with suppressed rage, pointed a trembling finger towards Edge. Truman, his right hand heavily bandaged, eyed the half-breed nervously.

'I got deputies at all the exits,' the sheriff warned as the mortician stooped over the dead girl and went through the motions of testing for a pulse and holding a piece of looking glass in front of her blood-run mouth.

'I shot her!' John Day said suddenly, jerking out of the trancelike state that had gripped him ever since he had seen the whore slide off the sofa.

Relief flooded Truman's fleshy face and he performed his quick draw technique with a finger under the buttons of his coat. His right holster was still empty but the Colt slid smoothly from the left and was jammed into the small of Day's back.

'It was accidental,' Elizabeth exclaimed as the Pitt endeavoured to hide her disappointment.

'Up to the court to decide,' Truman growled, confident he was now in control of a situation he had dreaded. 'Move it, son. Let go of him, ma'am.'

Elizabeth released her grip of John's arm. The mortician hummed a funereal hymn to himself as he took out a tape and began to measure the length and breadth of the corpse.

Day was suddenly struck by a frightening thought. He looked around the room with horror-filled eyes. 'Elizabeth!' he cried. 'Who'll take care of Elizabeth?'

'She can have the bedroom,' Haven replied. 'Miss Pitt will arrange to have a bed moved in here for me.'

'Not if you were the . . .' John began in a biting tone.

'I'll be all right, John,' the woman insisted.

'She may stay in my house behind the church,' the priest said.

'Edge!' Day exclaimed suddenly as Truman spun him

around and forced him out of the doorway. 'I charge you with her safety.'

'That guy's not a bad judge,' the man with the searching stare muttered.

'All I need is a place to stay,' Elizabeth said, looking at the madam. 'I can take care of myself.'

Millie Pitt shook her head emphatically. 'Sorry, dearie,' she said harshly. 'Even if I had the room, I wouldn't let you stay.'

'Nice girl like you would get the place a good reputation,' Edge put in as he began to roll a cigarette.

'Take her out with you when you leave,' the madam growled at Edge, then swung towards the mortician. 'And you hurry up and finish your work, Jem Potter. Pine with rope handles. Cynthia didn't hardly pay back the fare I laid out from New Orleans.'

'Best oak with gold trimmings,' Haven contradicted as the madam swept out of the room. 'Send the bill to me.' His sad eyes moved towards the priest. 'And a full funeral service. A choir and the death knell.'

The prospect of a higher profit margin urged the mortician to speed his work and hurry from the room to make the arrangements. The priest bobbed his head and followed Potter along the corridor. Elizabeth ran the tip of her tongue nervously along her lips as she tried to conceal the apprehension in her green eyes.

'My offer is still open, Miss Day,' Haven said sympathetically.

'Stick with Edge,' the well-dressed man of violence urged.

'Get lost, pint size,' the half-breed muttered around the cigarette slanting from the corner of his mouth.

'Be careful,' Haven warned as the small man formed his lips into the crooked semblance of a smile. 'Now that Hyman's dead, Jonas Pike is the only man in Summer you have to worry about, Edge.'

The half-breed's hooded eyes raked over the short man again. 'You're Jonas Pike?' he asked easily, trying to spot the tell-tale bulge of a concealed weapon in the well-tailored suit.

'You've heard of me?' Pike asked with only mild interest.

'We almost trod in each other's footprints once,' Edge supplied cryptically.*

Pike nodded, obviously failing to understand the significance of the comment, but indifferent to it. 'Stay out of mine this time,' he said softly. 'My need is greater than yours.'

Edge showed Pike his own brand of mirthless grin and let the expression suffice for his reply.

Pike bowed stiffly towards Elizabeth. 'You'll be best advised to accept the priest's invitation, Miss Day,' he said. 'Apart from his religious ethics, he's married and has two grown-up daughters. Your virtue will be safe while you're in the house. And if you need to step out and I'm available, I'll be happy to act as your escort.'

The woman seemed on the point of ignoring Pike's advice but was startled by a sudden full-throated roar from below, as if every man in the saloon had been pushed tight against hysteria.

'That'll be Fanny La Rue starting her strip-tease act, Miss Day,' Haven said earnestly. 'It's the high spot of the night. And after she's finished it isn't safe for a young girl to be on her own in Summer.'

'Seems the Dakotas is full of naked women today,' Edge murmured as he headed for the door.

'Beast!' Elizabeth hissed at him as she stepped out of his way, then turned to show a coy smile to Pike. 'If you'll be good enough to see me across to the reverend's house, sir, I'll be most appreciative,' she said.

'I can expect to be hearing from you, Mr Edge?' Haven called after the half-breed.

'Sooner or later,' he answered, pressing himself against the wall to allow the mortician and two pall-bearers to squeeze past with an ornate casket. 'How much?' he asked.

'For the coffin or the entire funeral service, sir?' Potter asked enthusiastically.

*See: Edge – California Killing.

'Whole package?'

'For the best of everything, five hundred dollars,' Potter said, rubbing his hands together. 'You wish to make provision, sir?'

'He ought to,' Edge said, pointing to where Pike was ushering Elizabeth Day through the doorway of Haven's sitting room.

'I'll stand it for you,' Pike said as the mortician and his helpers entered the room. 'I reckon I'll be able to afford it and it follows that if I can, you'll be in need of burial.'

The two men smiled at each other, but Elizabeth knew they were not joking for she could see the willingness – almost eagerness – to kill lurking behind their cold stares.

'Please take me out of this place, Mr Pike,' she said hurriedly, tugging at the man's arm. 'I'd like to visit John before we go to the church house.'

Edge stepped back against the wall once more and ushered the couple along the corridor towards the head of the stairs. As they went down and another roaring cheer sounded from below, a voluptuously built woman stepped out from a room. She was flushed and still patting her hair into shape as she collided with Edge. She stepped back in surprise as she saw the last remnants of the killer's instinct visible in his hooded eyes.

'Sorry, mister,' she blurted out.

Edge ran his eyes over the powdered swells of her breasts bunched high by the stiffening of her low-cut dress. The woman became aware of his interest and showed him a sorrowful expression.

'The Pitt says I've got to take care of the Colonel after what happened to Cynthia,' she said. She gave him a sad smile. 'I'd rather go with you.'

'Just looking,' Edge told her. 'I never buy what I can get for free. Which room was Cynthia's?'

'Thirty on the top floor,' she answered, resentful of his attitude. 'What do you want there?'

'Sleep,' he told her as Jem Potter led the way out of Haven's room, followed in slow step by the pall-bearers with a more weighty burden.

'Worry you?' Edge asked the woman as both pressed themselves against the wall to allow the short procession to pass by.

'A girl takes her chances in a town like Summer,' the woman answered with a philosophical shrug that threatened to extend her decolletage. 'It's a risk we take.'

'Yeah, guess so,' Edge agreed as he turned towards the stairway to the third floor of the hotel. 'Whore today, gone tomorrow.'

CHAPTER EIGHT

THE rowdiness of the saloon did not reach to third floor level and the small, sparsely furnished room that had been Cynthia's sleeping quarters was a peaceful refuge for a weary traveller. But Edge did not immediately make use of the narrow cot pushed back against one wall. New habits, if they are bred by constant danger out of suspicious distrust, die harder than old and he first gave the room a searching examination, noting the cheap lock on the door, the window that looked out on a sheer drop into September Street and the trapdoor in the ceiling. He dragged the bed out into the centre of the uncarpeted room and stood on it to loosen the time-warped wood of the door panel out of its frame. Then it swung up easily to provide access to the flat roof of the hotel. He could not close it properly again and a draught of frosty night air intruded.

There was water in the cracked pitcher on the bureau and he poured it into a chipped, unmatched basin. Thin ice clinked against the porcelain. He splashed water on to his stubbled face and it refreshed him but did nothing to dissuade the pressing need for sleep.

Still he ignored the physical necessity, until he had attended to a final chore dictated by a mind trained to consider every possibility. This involved checking his weapons. He had no shells to replace the shot fired by Truman from the Navy Colt so he had to be content with using the pillowcase from the bed to clean the handgun, then simply checking the action. He cleaned, reloaded and checked the Winchester. Finally, he used his gunbelt as a strop to hone the razor.

Only then, after laying the rifle on the floor within easy reach, and tucking the Colt under his thigh, butt outwards, did he stretch out full length on the bed. He was fully dressed except for his low-crowned hat, which he set upon his face, far enough back to allow him to see both the door and window by simply snapping open his eyes. Then he slept: the sleep of a man who knew his next breath might be his last, at a level of unconsciousness that was but a pin-drop away from full alertness.

So it was that he heard the foot-treads in the corridor, and the sixth sense which is self-preservation's strongest ally warned him that the man was coming to his door.

Edge opened his eyes before the doorknob turned. It rattled angrily. 'Damn nuisance,' a man muttered.

'Room's taken,' Edge called softly, not moving his hat.

'Can't be,' the man called back after a surprised pause. 'Lady who runs the hotel just rented it to me.'

'She ain't no lady,' Edge told him. 'You can't trust that kind. Go get your money back.'

'I sure will, mister,' came the reply, then in a suddenly anxious tone. 'But where will I stay the night? She said this was the only spare room in town.'

'Try Frank's Livery couple of blocks down on August,' Edge suggested, flexing his fingers to combat the cold from the draughty trapdoor. 'Comes high but it's probably warmer than this place. And it's got to be a whole lot safer.'

'Safer?' the man posed nervously.

'Sure,' Edge told him. 'If you don't move away from that door and let me get some sleep you're right in line to find out what I mean.'

His gulp sounded very loud. 'I'm going, mister, I'm going!' he yelled, and proved his intent by heavy footfalls as he hurried back down the corridor.

Edge sighed and sat up on the bed, tipping the hat back on his head. He holstered the Colt, picked up the Winchester and rose to unlock the door. Then he climbed on to the bed and reached up to push open the trap. He shoved his Winchester through the frame and hauled himself aloft. He closed the trap. He could see completely over the town, illuminated by the full moon and a million stars that seemed to be pasted upon the matt black sky. A layer of sparkling frost, thick enough to resemble a light snowfall, reflected the night light. It coated Edge's clothes, hair and three day stubble as he crouched on the roof blowing on his cupped hands.

Less than two minutes had been chipped from time when The Gates of Heaven's new guest returned along the corridor. But now he had reinforcements and Edge guessed that it was not his fist that thudded on the door, loud and demanding.

'Open up in there!' a man ordered gruffly 'Or make your peace.'

Edge continued to breath vaporised breath into his hands and look at the sparkling rooftops of the town. He did not flinch as a shot exploded, splintering through the door lock. A middle-aged man with watery eyes and a goatee beard entered the room in a stumbling run, shoved from behind by two broad-shouldered gunmen toting Remingtons.

'Ain't nobody here,' one of them said in disgust.

'Nobody's right,' the other answered, glaring at the cowering new guest. 'Reckon the drummer here just didn't have enough strength to turn the door handle, Bart.'

Bart gave a harsh laugh.

'I talked to him,' the disconcerted salesman insisted. 'He threatened me.'

Bart gave the statement mock consideration. 'That Cynthia knew all the tricks,' he said. 'I hear that one old-timer wasn't halfway round the world when his ticker gave out. Maybe that was his ghost you heard, feller.' He pointed the gun. 'Snuffed it, right there on that bed.'

The salesman blinked and eyed the bed nervously.

'Cost of a new lock will go on your bill,' Bart said as he led the way from the room and his partner jerked the door closed.

The salesman pressed a hand against the dent in the blankets made by Edge's body and felt the last vestiges of warmth. 'Hey!' he said in a half cry, taking a step towards the door.

'Yeah?' Edge replied softly as he yanked up the trap-door and squatted in the opening, pointing the Winchester.

The nervous drummer could take no more. The only light in the room came from the window and through the trapdoor and in this meagre moonglow Edge, coated from head to toe in white frost, appeared as a gruesome apparition. The man's breath hissed out in a gasp and he fainted, his slight body falling backwards across his valise.

Edge grinned and dropped down on to the bed, pulling the trapdoor closed behind him. His teeth chattered with the cold and he could not feel his feet. He glanced at the salesman, crumpled beside the bed, and slid under the blankets. For several minutes he continued to shiver, but gradually his natural body heat built up a resistence to the cold and his mind once more gained supremacy over his physical being.

The salesman groaned and Edge brought a hand from under the blanket and jabbed the muzzle of the Navy Colt into the man's neck.

'Summer ain't no ghost town, feller,' he whispered as the man took a sharp, gasping breath.

'What ... what ... do you ... you want?' the salesman stammered.

'Sleep,' Edge replied, moving the revolver so that the cold steel of its barrel rested across the man's cheek. 'But I sleep light. Best you stay awake, in case you fidget. I feel one move and you'll be as dead as the old timer. But it won't be so much fun.'

'I'm freezing,' the salesman complained as Edge used his free hand to push his hat over his face.

'You'll be colder when you're dead,' Edge told him, and closed his eyes.

68

Edge slept until dawn while the wretched salesman fought against his fatigue and the freezing temperature of the night. He had ridden a great many miles and the lights of Summer's Solar Circle had seemed the answer to a dream. But their promise of warmth and comfort had turned into a nightmare and he felt sure he was going to die, either from cold or a bullet.

The half-breed slit open his eyes and took a fraction of a second to orientate himself. 'You did a good job, feller,' he congratulated as he reset his hat on his head and pushed back the blankets, lifting the Colt from the salesman's cheek.

The man continued to stay pressed against the floor, as if frozen there. Edge stood up and indicated the bed.

'All yours.'

The man's watery eyes, small and reflecting his pain, examined the towering figure of Edge with disbelief.

'Blankets are cooling fast,' Edge said easily as he crossed to the bureau. The dirty water he had used for washing last night was crusted with ice again and he used the butt of the Colt to crack it. As he splashed the reviving water on to his face the salesman picked himself painfully from the floor and collapsed on to the bed. He had enough strength left to drag the blankets up to his chin.

Edge went to the window and had to chip the iced condensation from the glass before he could look out on to the frozen emptiness of September. The grey dawn had swept a blanket of low cloud across the sky that seemed to be clamping a depressing grip over the town.

'Good day for sleeping,' Edge said as he turned away from the window.

'I've got a job to do, mister,' the salesman replied. His voice was weak but colour was beginning to spread into the pale skin above his mottled grey beard.

'What you selling?' Edge asked.

'Mail order service. I've got to fill my quota in this territory today or I'll get fired.'

'Small town,' Edge told him. 'You can cover it on foot.'

The salesman eyed him suspiciously. 'What's that

69

supposed to mean, mister?' he asked.

'Guess your horse is stabled down at Frank's Livery?' Edge moved to the door.

The salesman tried to force a threatening tone into his voice. 'They hang people for stealing horses, mister.'

Edge's expression was bland as he swivelled the Winchester up to a right angle with his hip-bone and aimed it at the bed. 'For murder, too,' he said softly. 'I've got nothing to lose.'

'Take it!' the salesman said hurriedly. 'Chestnut mare. McClellan cavalry saddle for him. Tell them I said you could. Name's Mann.'

'Not the one from Laramie?' Edge asked.

'What?' He shook his head. 'I'm from Cedar City, Utah.'

'Different branch of the family, maybe,' Edge murmured as he went out of the room.

The Gates of Heaven was in the clutch of a deathly quietness, as if the staff and guests were in the midst of a period of mourning for the dead whore. Edge heard the first sound when he entered the saloon and he brought up the Winchester in a smooth reflex action. But it was just a drunk, sprawled out across two tables pushed together, snoring in a regular cadence.

Edge climbed over one of the curved bar counters, gathered a bottle of whiskey from the shelf and went through a doorway into the kitchen. The windows were shuttered and it was dark in there. He lit a lamp. Carefully, making no noise, he unfastened a closet door and helped himself to coffee, two cans of beans and some meat loaf. A tin mug completed his supplies and he put everything into a cook's apron and gathered the corners to form a bundle before he went out, by way of the kitchen door which gave on to September Street.

The light level of the new day had risen since he awakened but the biting cold had not receded and the frost crunched under his boots as he crossed the broad intersection of Solar Circle. An oil lamp still burned inside the County Bank but the Pinkerton guards had finished their card game.

They were sprawled out across the table in a sound sleep, hands curled around their rifles.

The gaolhouse with the sheriff's office beside it, was next door to the bank. A face appeared at the barred window of the gaol, almost as white as the frost on the streets and roofs.

'Edge!' John Day called.

The half-breed's facial muscles tightened, pulling his features into the shape of an angry snarl. He quickened his pace, angling across to the gaolhouse.

'You want me to run an ad. in the local paper, as well?' he rasped.

Day's homely face showed his confusion.

'To let the whole town know I'm leaving,' Edge explained coldly.

'Where's Elizabeth?' Day asked, his tone lowered to a whisper.

'With the preacher,' Edge told him.

'I don't trust that Pike man she was with last night,' Day said anxiously.

'Figure him for a real sharp feller myself,' Edge said, turning away.

'I charged you with her safety,' Day retorted, his tone rising.

'Right now I need a dame like I need a loud-mouthed gaolbird,' Edge shot back, spinning towards the window and bringing up the Winchester.

The stock stabbed between the bars and took Day full on the jaw. He gave a low groan and reeled back across the cell. He thudded against the far wall and slid down to the stone floor.

'Good, Day,' the half-breed murmured and moved back to his original course, heading down August towards the livery stables.

Smoke curled up into the freezing air from the chimney on the building with the big double doors and there was a light on inside. Edge cracked open one of the doors without knocking and stepped into the warmth on the other side. He looked down the bore of a Spencer and curled back his lips in a grin.

'Need a horse and saddle,' he said easily, holding the Winchester so that it was aimed at the dirt floor.

The gangling old man with the gaunt face who charged such a high rate, was seated in a rocker facing a pot-bellied stove which glowed red hot. His greedy eyes were as steady as the aim of the repeater as he looked at Edge through the rising heat from the stove.

'Just take care of 'em,' he replied. 'Don't sell 'em.'

'Been offered them on loan,' Edge said, advancing further into the stable, welcoming the warmth that set up a tingle in his fingertips. 'Drummer named Mann rode in last night. Won't be needing his chestnut mare today.'

There was now just the stove between them, but the stableman appeared unworried as he maintained the aim of the Spencer. 'Got authorisation from the feller?'

'You got my word it's the truth,' Edge replied.

'Ain't good enough.'

'Your misfortune,' Edge said and began to fall backwards. His feet came clear of the ground and were thrust forward. The heels of his boots thudded against the top of the stove in a double-footed drop-kick. The stove was uprooted on one side and as it tipped the chimney snapped free.

As the old man yelled and rocked backwards, burning logs spewed from the top of the stove. Edge was back on his feet and in a crouch as the chair rocked forward again. The old man's forehead smashed into the jagged tin of the severed chimney and opened up into a yawning gash. A curtain of pumping blood blinded his eyes as his bare feet plunged into the pile of spilled logs. He screamed, dropped the Spencer and leapt from the rocker. Then he sat down hard on the ground and used one hand to wipe blood from his eyes as the other beat at the smouldering cuffs of his levis.

Horses snorted and stamped their hooves as they smelt smoke. Keeping the old man covered, Edge backed over to the stalls and found the one with the right kind of saddle hanging outside. As he made to go inside, he saw the stableman reaching for the Spencer.

'You just don't know when you've had enough,' he said

with a sigh, getting to the man in three long strides.

The man cowered away from him, blinking rapidly to try to keep the blood out of his eyes. Although he was tall, he was thin and Edge was able to lift him with ease. Back at the stall he used the Winchester to knock the saddle down and then hoisted the struggling man aloft. He looped the man's belt over the hook and let go of him. The man was doubled over from the hook, dripping blood to the ground.

'You just signed your own death warrant,' he flung at Edge as the half-breed moved into the stall and began to saddle the chestnut mare. 'Frank ain't gonna like this.'

'Weren't done for Frank's enjoyment,' Edge told him, tightening the cinch. 'You should have accepted a man's word.' He attached the bridle and swung up on to the horse. 'Tell me something,' he said as he moved the animal gently out of the stall.

'You're getting nothing more from me,' the old man snarled defiantly.

Edge carefully reached up behind his neck and drew the razor. He had to lean down to brandish it in front of the man's face. 'See this?' A sharp intake of breath provided the answer. 'I can cut you down or I can cut your throat.'

'What d'you want to know?'

'River runs south of town.'

'Old Creek.'

'Any place around here it swings close to some other kind of wash?'

'Not that I know of. It forks about twenty miles west of here, though.'

'That better be the truth,' Edge said menacingly.

'I ain't in no position to lie,' the old man answered.

'Now I guess that is the truth,' Edge allowed and slashed with the razor. The recently honed blade sliced cleanly through the leather belt and the old man dropped heavily to the ground. His jaw collided with Edge's outstretched boot on the way down and he lay still.

Sliding the razor back in its neck pouch, Edge steered the nervous mare around the still smouldering logs and used the Winchester to prod open one of the doors. Hitting the

73

cold air was like running up against a tangible barrier. But the half-breed had the prospect of the reward money to keep him warm as he turned his mount towards the bridge over Old Creek.

From the second floor front window of his room, Jonas Pike watched Edge riding away from him. From such a distance, it was impossible to identify the figure, but the small man knew who the rider was. For he had been aware of Edge leaving the hotel, had seen him in conversation with John Day at the gaolhouse and watched him go into the livery.

'There goes one early bird who's after more than worms,' he said to himself as he turned from the window.

CHAPTER NINE

THE Creek flowed by turns rapidly and sluggishly from a source in the far distant north west so that the going was alternately flat and graded against Edge. But the chestnut mare was a younger and stronger animal than both the horses he had used to reach the town and she seemed to derive some form of equine satisfaction from widening the distance between her and the smoky warmth of the livery.

After a series of catty-cornered moves among a grotesque area of outcrops five miles from town, to ensure that he was not being followed, Edge allowed the mare to make her own pace, merely bringing her back on to the correct course whenever she took it into her head to wander away from the river bank.

Although the morning became brighter with the pale yellow of winter sun and the frost melted away into broad patches of wetness, it did not become noticeably warmer. Edge ate breakfast as he rode, breaking up the meat loaf in his cold-stiffened fingers. When Summer was lost amid its surrounding hills, the clear light served only to emphasise the empty wasteland formed by the eroded terrain. But although it was really one vast plain, it was not flat like the prairies of his native Iowa. It rolled in hummocks and dips, forming an erratic arrangement of convolutions like an ocean fossilised at the height of a storm.

The creek followed a line of least resistance through this Godforsaken stretch of country and since he stayed close to it, Edge was constantly in a long, meandering depression. He well knew that one band of Teton Dakotas had been gunning for whites and judged it a safe bet that there were more scalp-hunting parties in the area. So he avoided halting to boil coffee and even as he ate he kept a constant surveillance for Sioux sign.

From time to time he uncorked the whiskey bottle, enjoying the warmth which the raw liquid spread through his chest and across his stomach.

After two hours of easy riding, in which he covered a little more than ten miles, the creek narrowed suddenly and the water turned white as it was forced through a shallow gorge. Half a mile further on it disappeared underground. Edge halted his mount and took a long pull at the whiskey bottle as he contemplated the possibilities. Then he urged the mare up the incline of the nearest high ground and shaded his slit eyes with a hand as he surveyed the area ahead. He saw only another view of emptiness with not a single patch of brush or scrub to indicate the underground course of the water.

All he could do was to accept the stableman's directions at face value and continue to head westwards. He came down off the skyline and now had to take a firmer control on the reins since the mare had no clearly discernible course to follow.

The creek stayed below ground for more than two miles and then reappeared as little more than a gentle stream trickling along a trench at the centre of a broad bed. A scattering of rotting tree branches and water-smoothed boulders together with other debris indicated the kind of flooding strength which the creek commanded when it gathered the melting snow of the northern Black Hills in the spring.

The unwarm sun told of a time close to ten o'clock when Edge reached the point where the creek he had been following was joined by another curving in from the north. The wash was less than six feet across and only a few inches deep at the meeting point. Independently, the streams were mere trickles.

The creeks joined at the foot of two shallow valleys and formed another, slightly deeper one. On the northern slopes, sheltered to some extent from the high, biting winds of winter, a little brush and some tough grass grew in oddly shaped patches. It was at the side of this area that Jonas Pike was crouched, blowing at the tiny flame which had caught amid a pile of uprooted brush. His horse, ground hobbled and still saddled, chomped discontentedly at a patch of grass.

'What kept you, Edge?' Pike called without looking up from his chore.

Edge, with not a flicker of surprise, wheeled his horse towards Pike's camp and kept her down to a walk as he approached. The small man with the slight frame and strong eyes looked even more out of his element. On top of his eastern suit he had donned an ankle-length frock coat split up the back to the hips. It was an old coat, once black but now stained to many shades by long miles of travel. Most of his neatly-trimmed red hair was hidden by a derby tilted to a jaunty angle.

As Edge reached him, the fire caught and he straightened up, turning to treat the half-breed to a friendly smile. The fact that he was looking into the muzzle of a Winchester did not cause his good humour to waver.

'Coffee?' he asked.

Edge held his steady, easy gaze for a few seconds, then lowered the rifle and spat. 'If you're making it, I'll drink it,' he said as he slid out of the saddle. He tossed the bundle of supplies at the feet of the other man. 'Use mine,' he invited as he led his horse across to the meagre grazing.

'Plenty of my own,' Pike answered.

'Glad to know it,' Edge told him as he tethered the mare. 'Take care of my needs the rest of the way.'

The implied threat was ignored by Pike as he delved into his bedroll and drew out a coffee pot. 'Only one way to go from here,' he said, heading down to the bank at the meeting point of the streams. 'That's back to Summer,' He filled the pot and came back up the gentle slope. 'Whoever told you to come out here gave you a bum steer, mister.'

He set the pot down at the centre of the glowing brush and squatted beside the fire, watching Edge quizzically as the half-breed unsaddled the mare.

'I should have cut his throat,' Edge said, then clicked his tongue against the roof of his mouth. 'Maybe I will.'

'Dead men tell no tales,' Pike said with a shrug. 'But he's already told me.'

Edge sat down on the opposite side of the fire and watched Pike pour coffee into the pot. 'How much did it cost you?' he asked.

'I did him a favour and he did me one,' Pike answered.

'Friends that stick together ought to get stuck together,' Edge murmured, fingering the smooth handle of his razor, concealed beneath his long hair.

Pike dropped the amiable smile now, but his expression slid into neutral as he looked through the drifting smoke at Edge. 'Canyon where the army wagons were hit is a good seventy miles from here,' he said. 'What made you think you could pick up the trail at this fork?'

'My business,' Edge answered.

Pike nodded his acceptance of this, then stood up. Edge tightened his grip on the rifle, but held his easy pose as the small man crossed to his horse. 'Heard you ran into Hyman just before he died,' Pike said as he hooked a mug from his bedroll.

'That Day woman and the stableman ought to start a choir,' Edge muttered.

'She has a sweeter voice,' Pike said with a grin as he returned to his place.

The aroma of boiling coffee was strong in the clear air.

Pike picked the pot up with a gloved hand and poured steaming blackness into the mug Edge extended. Edge added a slug of whiskey to his own drink.

'May I?' Pike asked, holding out his mug.

Edge shrugged and poured him a shot. 'Man in your position ought to have his final request granted,' he said.

Pike took off his gloves and warmed his hands around the mug. 'You're determined you're going to kill me?' he asked casually.

Edge nodded and sipped the scalding coffee. 'You need Haven's reward too much, feller,' he answered. 'Maybe as much as I figure I need it. Last time I got close to ten grand I lost out.* This time it ain't going to be like that.'

The Winchester had been resting across Edge's folded legs. Now, as he sipped the coffee, he used his free hand to move the rifle so that it was aimed through the fire to where Pike was squatting. The small man was also drinking the coffee with one hand. The other was in a deep pocket of his long coat.

'In cold blood?' Pike asked, showing no sign of apprehension.

'I'm the lazy type,' Edge answered casually. 'Take the easy way every time.'

Pike shook his head. 'I'll go the easy way, Edge,' he corrected. 'You hit me anywhere vital with a bullet from that Winchester and I'm dead.' He sipped more coffee and smacked his lips. 'Now what I'm holding in my left hand is a little old Remington point three-six. I'd have to hit you plumb in the middle of your heart to kill you right off. I'm just not that good with a handgun. Dying won't come easy for you.'

Pike moved his hand in the pocket, so that Edge could see he was not bluffing. A revolver was outlined by the material of the long coat. The two men eyed each other steadily through the rising smoke for several long moments. But then the brooding silence of the Badlands was pierced by a sound—the harsh, forced laughter of a woman. By

*See: *Edge – Ten Thousand Dollars American.*

78

tacit agreement, both men were able to look away, each sure that the other would not fire.

The smaller man showed surprise as he recognised Elizabeth Day leading her horse down the slope towards the camp, her teeth gleaming in amusement, her red hair sheened by the bright, cold sunlight. Edge gave her a mere glance, then swung his hooded eyes back towards Pike and squeezed the Winchester's trigger.

Pike grunted and fell to the side, jerking the Remington from his pocket. His expression became a mixture of shock and rage as the gun dropped from his numbed fingers and he looked down at the bloody furrow across the back of his hand. As Elizabeth shouted Edge's name, Pike rolled, reaching out his good hand for the gun. Edge, still squatting in a relaxed posture, altered the aim of the rifle. A bullet sent the Remington spinning away from Pike's outstretched fingers.

'I'm pretty good with a rifle,' the half-breed said softly. 'It can be slow for you.'

'Stop it!' the woman shrieked, closing in on the men at a run. 'You'll kill each other.'

'Quick on the uptake, ain't she?' Edge asked Pike.

Pike got slowly to his feet and used his good hand to doff his hat to the woman. 'It has to be one of us, Miss Day,' he said lightly. 'Your untimely arrival seems to have given the advantage to him.'

'Don't blame the dame,' Edge told him, easing himself upright, careful to keep the rifle aimed at Pike. 'Your mistake.'

Pike nodded. 'In trusting a man like you.'

Edge shrugged. 'Man's never too old to learn. But I reckon that lesson came too late in your life, feller.'

'Drop your gun, Mr Edge,' Elizabeth commanded sharply.

Again Edge merely glanced at her before returning his concentration towards Pike. She was pointing the pepper-box at him from a range of less than six feet. Her hand was shaking, but he realised she had probably been more scared when she shot the Sioux brave.

'You've seen what I can do with this,' she said coldly, as if reading his mind.

'What's he to you?' Edge asked.

'As much as you,' she answered. 'Not much, but the best of a bad bunch. I don't want to shoot you, Mr Edge, but I will unless you drop the rifle.'

Pike smiled with his mouth. 'I think she means it, Edge,' he warned.

'I know she does,' Edge answered and allowed the Winchester to clatter to the hard, frozen ground.

'And your gunbelt,' Elizabeth pressed.

Edge pursed his lips in a silent whistle as he unbuckled the belt and allowed it to fall, the holstered Colt striking the rifle barrel. A motion with the Ladies Companion urged both men to back away from their fallen weapons. She used a foot to drag the guns into an untidy heap.

'You have no other firearms, Mr Pike?' she asked.

He touched his hat brim. 'You have my word, ma'am.'

She nodded her acceptance of this and gave a short sigh of relief, followed at once by a tight-lipped smile. 'Now we can talk turkey,' she said.

'Carved up three ways?' Edge suggested.

'I saved the life of one of you,' she answered. 'Why, for goodness sake, you could have killed each other. It's not too much to ask.'

'Virtue is its own reward, Miss Day,' Pike quoted. 'You did what you thought was right and now you'd better leave things as they are. The gesture was commendable, but useless I'm afraid.'

He raised his injured hand to his mouth and sucked gently at the wound. His eyes locked upon those of Edge. 'Not only guns, uh?' he asked, his tongue licking blood from his lips.

'What do you think, feller?' Edge asked, taking a half step towards Pike.

'That you aren't as stupid as you look,' Pike replied and took a half step of his own.

'Stop it!' Elizabeth pleaded, waving the tiny gun between the two men. 'You're both stupid.'

It was as if neither man heard her words. They approached each other with measured slowness, halting a yard apart, on the far side of the dying fire from the woman.

'Time to carve?' Pike asked softly.

'It's the man's job,' Edge answered. As he spoke the final word, his right hand shot to the back of his neck in a blur of movement. It emerged from beneath his long hair only a split-second later. The blade of the razor had a murderous glint in the bright sunlight.

The woman gasped, at his speed and in exasperation that she had forgotten about this weapon. She pointed her tiny gun at Edge but the compulsion to fire was swamped by a more forceful demand not to.

Pike went down into a stoop, as if to duck under a thrust from the razor. But the movement was merely the first stage in a lightning attacking stratagem of his own. His good hand disappeared for a moment through a split in his pants at calf level. When it emerged, it was clutching a wooden-handled knife with a six-inch stiletto blade. As he straightened the double-edged weapon bounced sunlight into the half-breed's eyes.

'Goodness!' the woman exclaimed and threw her hands up to her face as the knife was thrust towards Edge's stomach.

'But no mercy,' Edge muttered as he side-stepped and slashed the razor crosswise.

Pike grunted and jerked his head back. The razor nicked the tip of his nose and blood oozed.

'Should have kept it out of my business,' Edge told him coldly as he went into a half crouch, moving his body slowly to left and right.

'Money is my business, mister,' Pike shot back, and leapt at his man.

Edge's reflexes, honed sharper than the razor, sent his body into a sideways arch. His arm moved and the razor slashed again, this time towards Pike's throat. But the smaller man was just as fast. His free hand sprang up, his forearm blocking the slash. The knife was turned by a snapping wrist action. Instead of stabbing into Edge's

6

stomach, it sliced through his pants and cut a narrow gash in the lean flesh of his hip.

'Please!' the woman screamed, looking at the two men through the cracks between her fingers.

Edge dropped his left arm with force, trapping Pike's knife hand against his injured side. He grinned down into the surprised face of the smaller man, but an instant later knew Pike was faking. For as he drew back the razor to slash it in an arc under the other's defence, Pike brought up his knee.

White hot pain exploded from Edge's groin and sent burning sparks to every nerve in his body. He staggered backwards and the knife was jerked free. The blade cut through his coat and shirt sleeve and sliced deep into his upper arm. He fought to stay on his feet, to keep Pike in his agony-blurred vision as he stumbled in involuntary retreat from the smaller man's advance. But the heel of his boot stepped into the tin coffee mug and he fell. He flailed his arms and saw the sky reel above him. For a blinding moment he stared full into the sun. Then his back jarred against the ground and a fresh wave of pain gripped him with an immobilising force.

'Leave him!' Elizabeth shrieked. 'You've beaten him.'

Pike slowed his advance, but there was no lessening of intent upon his weathered face as he spun the knife in the air and caught it by the tip. 'Only one way he'll ever admit to it, ma'am,' he said softly.

He threw the knife.

Elizabeth fired the gun.

Edge rolled.

The half-breed's mind was tossing in a broiling sea of agony that was his body. He neither saw the knife coming at him nor heard the tiny crack of the gun. But that instinct for self-preservation which had kept him alive through so many violent years, snapped him into action.

The knife was buried to the hilt in the ground which an instant before had been warmed by Edge's body.

Pike yelled in pained surprise as the bullet grazed the nape of his neck.

Elizabeth gasped and stared in horror at the smoking pepperbox. 'Oh, my goodness!' she exclaimed.

Pike lunged full-length at Edge, both hands reaching for the razor. Edge had rolled full circle and saw his attacker as a shadowy form in front of the sun. Then the shadow gained substance as Pike's weight crashed on top of him. As Pike's fingers locked upon his right wrist, Edge swung his left arm in a powerful half circle. He chopped the man hard across the back of the neck. Pike revealed his pain only by a sudden rush of expelled breath which was hot against Edge's face.

Locked together, both men rolled. First one way and then the other. Edge kept his arm tight around Pike's neck as Pike sought to wrench the razor free. Blood from their wounds stained their clothes and the ground. Their breathing became ragged. By turns, each tried to stand, but neither was prepared to allow the other the advantage of height, even for a split-second.

'Stop it at once, or I'll . . .' The woman's pretty face, drained of colour, was suddenly contorted by indecision as she looked about her, searching for a tangible threat. Then her frightened eyes settled upon the men's tethered horses. She released the reins of her own mount and hoisted her skirts to run across to the contentedly grazing animals. 'Or I'll turn them loose!' she finished.

The men did not hear her.

Pike was twisting his hands in opposite directions around Edge's wrist. Edge gritted his teeth against the burning pain, but was forced to release his grip on the razor. Pike started a sigh of satisfaction, but it ended as a startled cry as the half-breed's body bucked beneath him. He was freed at the neck and rose several inches into the air. As he dropped, Edge's left fist smashed into the side of his jaw. His head slammed into his shoulder and he collapsed limply on to the hard leanness of the half-breed's body.

'I warned you!' Elizabeth yelled with a sob in her voice. 'You can't say I didn't!'

She stooped and fumbled with trembling fingers at the tethers. Edge snaked his pain-wracked body out from beneath the dead weight of Pike and started to scramble to his feet. But Pike recovered an instant too soon and clutched at the half-breed's ankles, jerking him over again. As Edge sat down hard, Pike released him and sprang on to his haunches, then upright. Edge was only a moment behind him in gaining his feet.

'I warned you!' the woman shrieked and stood between the two horses to slap them hard on their hindquarters.

The animals snorted in protest, reared and bolted. They galloped full-tilt down the slope, directly towards the two men. The sound of their hoofbeats unlocked the stare of cold hatred that linked their glinting eyes. Each man saw the animals bearing down upon him and sprang back out of their path. The horses streaked between them and their headlong dash spooked the woman's mount. It wheeled and raced in pursuit.

Edge and Pike watched the three animals splash across the river fork and then race up the incline on the other side, to disappear over the rise. Within moments the sound of their hoofbeats had faded into the distance. The two men looked at each other again. The killer glint had left their eyes and the tension had drained from their bodies.

'Bad enough the way we are,' Pike suggested.

Blood was crusted on his nose and around his mouth. He put a hand to the back of his neck and his fingers came away coated with fresh, red moisture. There was an ugly bruise on his jaw.

'A better time and a better place,' Edge agreed.

His coat sleeve and pants leg were stained by dried blood.

'I did warn you,' Elizabeth said meekly as both men turned to look at her. She tried to hold their cold stares, but was forced to hang her head. 'Perhaps we can catch them?' she tried.

Edge jerked a thumb over his shoulder. 'They went thataway,' he snarled. 'I reckon you'll be able to run faster if you shed a few of those fancy clothes.'

Elizabeth caught her breath as Edge took a step towards her. Then she remembered she was still holding the pepperbox and she jerked it up. 'What do you mean?' she demanded.

Edge continued to move towards her, pushing a hand inside the slit in his pants. When he withdrew it the fingers and palm were shiny with new blood. He halted a yard from her and held up his hand, bunched into a fist.

'Edge!' Pike yelled threateningly.

Edge opened his hand fast and droplets of blood sprayed across the woman's face. She let out a horrified howl and dropped the tiny gun so she had both hands free to scrub at her face.

'I'm bleeding, lady!' Edge snarled at her.

Pike approached her now, but his mundanely handsome face did not reflect Edge's hatred. And his tone was soft, understanding. 'We need to have our wounds dressed, Miss Day,' he explained. 'Nothing we're wearing is suitable for bandages.'

Relief flooded her pretty face and she nodded vigorously, anxious to help. 'If you'll just turn your backs for a moment,' she replied.

Edge shook his head. 'No, lady,' he told her. 'Somebody as stupid as you needs to be watched the whole time. I let you out of my sight and maybe you'll whip up more trouble.'

'What could I possibly do, for goodness sake?' she asked.

'You'll think of something,' Edge told her. 'Get them off!'

'Don't be so crude!' she snapped in reply, but stooped to reach under the dress for her petticoats. She stepped out of them delicately, ensuring they did not fall to the ground.

'Shall I do it?' Pike asked, reaching out his good hand.

She gave the frothy white garment to him and as he began to tear the material into strips, Edge backed away and gathered up his discarded weapons. Pike watched him without appearing to do so, tense for a few moments. But then, as the tall half-breed carefully pushed the razor into its neck pouch and squatted down to check the actions of the guns, he relaxed as much as the pain allowed. He still did not trust Edge, but realised that for some reason of his own, the man with the cruel face and killer's instinct was prepared to honour the truce.

For his part, Edge trusted the smaller man implicitly, for he had revised his opinion of him. Pike was not like himself. He was tough, strong, fast and smart. He was also a killer. But whatever force of circumstances had led him along the trail of violence, it had not stripped him of every vestige of humanity. He continued to cling to a shred – perhaps even the whole canvas – of a code of honour. This was what made him different from Edge, and diminished him as an adversary in the half-breed's eyes.

Pike worked skilfully and quickly at transforming the woman's underwear into bandages and dressings. She, still intent upon making restitution for her action in scaring off the horses, obeyed his politely spoken instructions without complaint. She built up the fire, then washed the coffee pot clean of dregs before filling it with fresh creek water and placing it amid the flames.

'Edge first,' Pike said as she tried to examine his neck wound.

Edge had sat quietly smoking as he watched the activity, a pensive frown upon his leathery features. He reached for the whiskey bottle and took a swig before allowing Elizabeth to ease off his sheepskin jacket and roll up the sleeve to reveal the arm wound.

'You'd better save some of that to disinfect the wounds,' Pike suggested evenly.

Edge nodded and corked the bottle, then watched as, following Pike's instructions, the woman cleaned his wounds. She had some difficulty with the cut on his hip since she tried not to see too much of the exposed flesh when she had eased his pants down away from the wound. But she managed it as gently as she could. Then she poured whiskey on to pads and bound up both wounds with bandages.

She went through the same procedure with the ugly-looking bullet wounds on Pike's hand and neck and then cleaned up the blood from his cut nose. Edge noticed, with a feeling he was annoyed to identify as resentment, that she took greater care with the smaller man's injuries.

'We didn't lose too much blood,' Pike said when Elizabeth had completed her nursing chore. 'But it's a long walk back. We'll have to take it slowly and rest regularly.'

'You talk like a doctor,' Elizabeth said, surprised, as she smoothed out her dress, trying to get the skirts to hang properly without a petticoat beneath.

'And acts like one, some of the time,' Edge put in as he got to his feet, buckling his gunbelt and resting the Winchester across his shoulder.

Pike showed them his crooked smile. 'I don't practise anymore,' he said. 'You won't be getting a bill, Edge.'

Edge hung his own brand of mirthless humour on his stubbled face. 'You'll get paid, feller,' he answered.

'A better time and a better place?' Pike quoted back to the half-breed.

Elizabeth felt the tension between the two men, and saw the latent anger behind their cold eyes. 'I wish I hadn't run the horses off,' she said quickly. 'I had some food in my saddlebags. I'm hungry.'

'We'll all be a lot hungrier by the time we reach town,' Pike told her, but took the implied rebuke from his tone with a gentle smile. He glanced around at the barren terrain. 'No chance of finding anything to eat out here. But there's plenty of water.' He glanced at Edge. 'If we take the long way back.' He drew no response from the half-breed. 'Keeping out the cold is going to be our biggest problem,' he concluded, buttoning the high collar of his coat.

Elizabeth snatched up the whiskey bottle from the ground. 'This will help!' she shouted excitedly. But then disappointment spread across her face as she saw the meagre contents of the bottle. 'Goodness, there's only a mouthful left.'

Edge sighed and turned to move down to the bank of the creek. 'Seems like one swallow's going to have to make Summer,' he tossed back at them.

CHAPTER TEN

NIGHT had re-established its freezing grip on the ill-named town when the cold, empty-bellied trio crossed the rickety tressle bridge and started up August Street. That element of the local citizenry which frowned upon the money-hungry transients that Haven's offer had attracted had already retreated behind the barred doors and shuttered windows of their houses. But the lights of Solar Circle were shining their expensive welcome to weary travellers and the noise of those enjoying the pleasures inside The Gates of Heaven had a pleasing ring after the unaltering silence of the Badlands.

They had talked little on the long walk following the water course: Edge not at all and Pike and Elizabeth Day only when it was absolutely necessary.

'I don't owe you anything, Edge,' Pike said softly as they crossed the intersection at August and July and saw the charred ruins of Frank's Livery.

'You owe me, feller,' Edge shot back in the same key. 'For the trouble you caused leading Miss Goody Twoshoes out there.'

Elizabeth seemed about to say something, but realised that she had apologised enough. They had forgiven her to the extent of leaving her unharmed and she could expect nothing more from such men as these.

Pike nodded. 'Okay. So I'm not doing you a favour. I'm repaying a debt by telling you to keep looking over your shoulder in this town.'

The half-breed's teeth shone in the lights from Solar Circle. 'You wouldn't shoot a man in the back, doc,' he said.

'Not me,' Pike said with a shake of his head. 'I patched up the liveryman after you'd worked him over. His name's Brad Rivers. Related by marriage to Frank Chandler, who owns that burned building. Rivers was explicit about what Chandler would do to you if you ever came back to Summer.'

They were almost at Solar Circle now, but August Street although lined on this block by stores and businesses premises still open, continued to harbour areas of darkness. Pike's words and the tone in which he spoke them caused Elizabeth to peer hard into the shadows and her imagination saw menace in every looming shape.

She swallowed hard. 'I think we should get off the street,' she urged.

'You should never be allowed on it,' Edge told her coldly.

She swung around to face the half-breed, her mind forming an angry insult to fling at him. But the events of the past two days caught up with her. She had not realised, until this instant, the strength of the strain under which she had been living since she had first set eyes on the man called Edge. She had always considered herself a woman with more than the average quota of common sense, able to adapt to each new circumstance with practical acceptance. But what had happened to her since she had looked up from her morning bathe and seen Edge ride around the bluff was too much for a well-brought-up woman to endure without giving way to natural feminine emotions. And because she had kept these at bay for so long, when the breaking point was reached, it was a dramatic one.

They were standing in front of the lighted window of the Cathay Restaurant and had an audience of three broadly grinning Chinese waiters.

'You filthy, rotten, stinking, cross-bred sonofabitch!' the woman screamed and flung herself at Edge, her fingers contorted into talons and her eyes gleaming with new-born tears.

As Elizabeth launched herself towards Edge he bobbed to the side and jerked back. Two rifle shots cracked together. Glass shattered and the woman screamed. One of the waiters took both bullets between the eyes and a fountain of his blood splashed across the shards of window glass in a wide arc as he fell. A second waiter's face was transformed into a horrific pulp of pumping redness as a spray of gleaming splinters showered at him. He whirled and started to scream in a high pitch as he staggered blindly among the panicked diners.

Out on the sidewalk Pike went full-length to the rough boards and fired the Remington with his unbandaged hand, aiming into the shadowed façade of the Summer Sun newspaper office. Edge got off one shot with the Winchester before the woman crashed into him. But terror had replaced her anger and she clung to him instead of fighting him. Her tears were warm and salty on his lips as her forehead made harsh contact with his nose.

The force of her lunge knocked him backwards through the half-open door of the restaurant and she was dragged inside after him. Two more rifle shots exploded from the newspaper office and the bullets dug wood splinters out of the doorframe.

'Obliged,' Edge hissed in her ear. 'You had to do something right some time, lady.'

'I . . .' she started, but Edge gave her no time to finish.

She yelled at the pain as he wrenched her hands free and went into a crouch at the side of the shattered window.

'Edge?' Pike called. 'I think this is your fight.'

A single shot came from across the street and Edge straightened and pumped three back before withdrawing into cover. 'I didn't ask for no help,' he answered.

A fusillade of shots cracked and glass and wood splinters skimmed over Edge's head. Elizabeth yelled as one stung her ankle and then she scuttled towards the back of the room where the staff and patrons were huddled.

'Well either get shot or finish off your playmates. My gun's as empty as my stomach.'

'Door's open,' Edge told him. 'So's the window. The Chop Suey smells good.'

'It must be full of ground glass,' Pike tossed back, then flattened himself against the sidewalk as a volley of rifle fire sounded and bullets whistled over his prone body.

'So stay out there and taste the lead,' Edge yelled, rising to empty the Winchester in a burst of rapid-fire.

Pike took advantage of the covering fire to belly towards the shattered window. Then he rose up on to all fours and leapt through, sprawling across the floor beside the half-crouched figure of the half-breed.

'Add chicken to the menu,' Edge called towards the cowering group at the rear of the restaurant as he ducked back into cover and began to pump a fresh load into the Winchester.

Pike stayed on the floor, close to the grotesquely crumped body of the dead Chinese and looked at the apparently cold expression on the face of Edge. And just as, earlier, Edge had reassessed the character of Pike, so now the smaller man reviewed his impression of the half-breed. He looked through the thin shell of coolness which cloaked the lean face like an insubstantial barrier and saw the controlled heat which burned behind. And he knew that Edge was not a cold-blooded killer. He was a professional who enjoyed his work: a man who did not really come alive until he was pointing a loaded gun in the right direction. He had to have an excuse to kill, but when the opportunity arose he was driven to take it by an inner slow-burning emotion close to ecstasy.

'Noodles, chow mein, sweet and sour pork and beef with bamboo shoots,' the half-breed hissed at Pike as he levered a shell into the breech. 'And a double portion of rice.'

'You're going somewhere?'

Edge nodded. 'But I'll be back. And I'll be hungry,'

He stayed down for a few more moments, until four shots had whistled in through the shattered window to thud into the wall. Then he leapt through the jagged edges of glass, the Winchester bucking in his hands. He hit the sidewalk lightly and sprang into the street. Then he ran, swerving to left and right, working the lever action and squeezing the trigger in a blur of wrist and finger movement. He received a fleeting impression of a large crowd gathered against the bright lights of Solar Circle: of a face here and there – Truman impassive, the Pitt smiling in enjoyment, the drummer, Mann, scared. And he was aware of the silence which gripped the downtown area, strange because it was so completely out of character with what Summer had become.

Only the sound of the Winchester exploding in his hand shattered the peace.

Then he leapt up on to the opposite side-walk and flattened himself against the front wall of the newspaper office. Rifles cracked from inside, biting chips of wood from the glassless window frame. Edge drew the Colt and snapped off three shots into the office before drawing back and feeding more shells into the Winchester.

'You burned down my place, Edge!' a man snarled from inside.

'And treated me bad,' the liveryman yelled.

Edge curled his thin lips back further to widen his grin. The level of the angry voices told him his rush across the street had driven Chandler and Rivers into the back of the office. His hooded eyes raked across to the front of the restaurant and he saw it was rapidly emptying as the people inside were herded into the kitchen at the back. Then he looked down into Solar Circle at the silently excited crowd and could sense the massed will of the witnesses demanding he be killed.

'Times are tough all round,' Edge called into the office, glancing over his shoulder to where an alley went between the newspaper office and a hardware store.

'You won't be living through any more,' Chandler called. 'Good or bad.'

He punctuated the threat with a shot, but Edge had moved away from the side of the window. He reached the mouth of the alley on the balls of his feet and stooped down to pick up a pebble. Gently, he lobbed it into the darkness, then whirled and got back to the window as silently as he had left it. He heard the pebble glance off the side wall of the building and drop to the ground: then a sharp intake of breath from within.

'He's goin' around back,' the liveryman whispered fearfully.

'Come on,' Chandler urged in low key.

There was a scuffling sound from inside as the two men turned to cover an attack from the rear. Edge stepped in front of the window and fired at the noise.

He saw them in the gun flashes. Rivers took the first shot in the shoulder and spun around, flinging aside his Spencer and gaping his mouth in a scream. Chandler caught a bullet in his hip and his Winchester went off, shattering his own foot.

Edge altered his stance, resting a shoulder against the window frame and taking careful aim with his cheek against the stock. He fired at each man in turn. Once in the groin, then in the stomach: and finally he killed them with bullets in their hearts as they writhed in the slippery pools of their own blood. The final cracks of the rifle, ending the men's high, thin screams, prefaced a silence that seemed to endure for an eternity and to deepen with each split-second.

'They dead?' Truman's voice boomed from out of the crowd.

Edge struck a match and reached in through the window to light a kerosene lamp standing on a desk. His slitted eyes, like tiny lengths of waxed blue cotton in the dark brown lids, examined the still forms sprawled in the blood.

'They sure don't look too healthy,' he replied in a normal tone. But the town was so still his voice carried to the crowd with ease.

A man broke out from the front row and hurried down August. It was the mortician in his high crowned hat and frock coat. He halted beside Edge and peered in at the blood-soaked tableau. 'I'm glad you left enough of them to inter,' he said wryly.

Edge looked into the newspaper office again and tried to understand it himself. The first two shots had been blind but then he had had the men fixed. He could have finished them with one more shot each. But something had driven him to make them die the hard way.

The answer wasn't with them. They were just a couple of trigger happy bushwhackers who had good reason to hate him. He looked down at Solar Circle, where a piano had started to jangle in The Gates of Heaven and the crowd was dispersing to pick up the action where it left off. It hadn't been for any of them, either. They already knew that nobody tangled with Edge without being aware of the risks.

It wasn't until he started across the street towards the bullet-scarred façade of the Cathay Restaurant that Edge discovered the reason for his actions. Jonas Pike was holding open the door for a pale-faced Elizabeth Day to pass through. When she was on the sidewalk he held out his arm and she took it gratefully.

Edge kept his expression impassive as he approached the couple, but behind his blank stare his mind was in a turmoil. Men – and women – had died by his hand for less trouble than this pretty, green-eyed redhead had caused him. But he had never so much as laid a finger on her. And it was because their ambush of him had put her life in danger, that Rivers and Chandler had been made to die so badly.

'I thought you'd come back,' Pike said. 'So I placed your order.'

Elizabeth met Edge's cold stare for a moment, then cast her eyes down. 'I'm sorry for what I said,' she whispered. Then: 'Please Mr Pike. Let's go and see how John is.'

There was a glint of triumph in Pike's smile as he nodded to Edge and escorted the woman down towards Solar Circle. The diners whose meal had been so violently interrupted now began to crowd out through the doorway, but pulled back sharply as the tall, lean, hard-faced half-breed bore down upon them.

Inside, a Chinese woman with the wrinkled skin of many years, was delicately picking glass slivers from the blood-run face of the injured waiter. His dead colleague was being lifted out through the window by two more women, younger, sobbing their grief.

'You eat your meal in kitchen, Mr Edge?' a Chinese in a starched shirt asked as he constantly bobbed his head. 'It warmer there. And no mess like dining room.'

Edge nodded and went through the door which was held open for him. It wasn't until he was in the steamy, over-heated atmosphere being ushered to a ready set table that he recalled how cold it was outside. And how cold he was after the gruelling walk. It was as if, ever since the first shots had announced the ambush, almost hitting Elizabeth Day, he had dropped out of reality into a world where the

94

lust for vengeance cancelled out every other sensation.

He sat tacitly at the table, unaware of the fearful sub-servience with which the cook and proprietor prepared and served his meal. It was characteristic of him that, having accepted what fate had thrust upon him, he did not attempt to explain it to himself. It had happened and he was stuck with it, period.

'I was hoping that when you left town, you wouldn't come back, Edge,' Sheriff Truman said from the doorway.

Edge looked up and across the steaming dishes of Chinese food towards the lawman. He saw no threat in his posture and began to eat. 'I don't figure to be around Summer for much longer,' he said through a mouthful of noodles.

'That's good news,' Truman answered. 'It seems that wherever you show up there's trouble. Whenever I see you, I start to sweat.'

Edge raked his eyes over the cook as he damped down the oven fire; at the proprietor hovering in case he was needed; and settled them on the unhappy face of the lawman. Then he shrugged. 'Little homily you might care to remember, Sheriff Truman.' He drew the Colt slowly and rested it on the table top, aimed at the bulky figure in the doorway. 'If you can't stand the heat, stay out of the kitchen. Now beat it, feller.'

Truman scowled, but turned and went out.

'Meal okay, Mr Edge?' the proprietor asked deferentially.

'Seems to be just what the doctor ordered,' the half-breed answered.

CHAPTER ELEVEN

THE noise made by the revellers in The Gates of Heaven reached the kitchen of the Cathay Restaurant as a low, discordant rumble. As Edge finished his meal and rolled a cigarette, it was the only sound in the small room, heavy with the stale odours of day long cooking. He was alone, the proprietor having retired to his sleeping quarters above the restaurant after sending his staff to their hovels in the poor section of Summer at the eastern end of September Street.

So when the harsh roar of an explosion ripped through the night there was no one to see the puzzled frown on his face. Nor to watch as he lit the cigarette, picked up the Winchester and strolled casually through the doorway into the dining room. As he stepped out through the shattered window, lights began to show along the entire length of August and shouted enquiries filled the silence which had followed the explosion.

Down on Solar Circle black smoke drifted lazily up from the front of the Summer County Bank. A man was calling for God's mercy. The doors of The Gates of Heaven Saloon facing the Circle burst open and a group of drunken men burst out on to the sidewalk. Rifle fire sounded in an angry burst and two of the men stumbled and sprawled into the intersection, already lightly powdered with night frost. The others in the group struggled with each other to get back inside the saloon.

'And I wasn't anywhere near the place, sheriff,' Edge muttered as he ducked into an opening between the black-smith and the express office.

'Jesus, they're knocking over the bank!' a man in a nightshirt yelled to his neighbour.

'I hope they get away,' a woman replied sourly.

'Right,' a dignified old man agreed. 'With no money to keep them here that scum will leave town.'

It was a four man gang. All young, all drunk and all broke. They had arrived in Summer over a period of two weeks, strangers to each other. As was the case with so many of the gunslingers who came to take up Haven's offer, the pleasures of The Gates of Heaven combined with the rumours of stirred up Sioux in the Badlands, was sufficient to cause them to postpone the hunt.

But their stakes were small and their luck turned sour at

the gambling tables. It was Bob Martin, a small-time horse thief from Texas who originated the idea – that it would be easier to simply steal the money from the bank rather than risk being scalped by Indians or shot up by the Ball gang to earn it honestly.

The details of the plan were hatched in a back room of the hotel that afternoon, in collaboration with three other youngsters. There was Hal Crane, a bank clerk on the run for embezzlement: Ed Baker wanted for the murder of his mistress's husband; and Joe Corners a novice bounty-hunter.

They pooled what was left of their bankrolls to buy enough red eye to get drunk and then had their first piece of luck since riding into Summer. For the unexpected gun-fight at the newspaper office held the attention of the entire town and allowed Martin and Corners to stroll into the September Street Gunshop and carry out a sackful of ammunition and dynamite while the storekeeper watched the shooting.

They were simple-minded men and it was the lack of complexity that got them into the bank without trouble. As Corners and Baker stood on the sidewalk, pleading with the stone-faced Pinkerton men to be allowed in to see the reward money, Martin and Crane forced a door at the rear. The hell-raising in the saloon across the Circle covered the sounds of their progress through the bank and the guards were sapped from behind before they could even suspect a raid.

Although they were drunk, inclined to be clumsy and to grin and giggle at their hamfistedness, their luck held for a little longer. They placed a charge of dynamite against the door of the big safe and set the cap without anybody in the town being aware of what was happening. This included Sheriff Truman, John Day, Elizabeth and the priest in the gaolhouse next door.

Then the dynamite exploded: and their luck ran out. The safe door blew off and its jagged edge sliced into Corners' right leg, severing it just below the knee before smashing into and through the wall. As smoke filled the room, foul-smelling and eye-burning, the injured man clutched at the meaty stump of his leg and peered desperately through the billowing clouds for the missing part. Then the agony hit him and he began to scream for relief.

'Goddamit!' Martin yelled, running for the gaping hole in the wall and leaning into it, thrusting his Winchester through. 'What a way to build a bank.'

Then his mouth dropped open as his whiskey-befuddled brain reasoned the explanation. His rifle swung to and fro, covering the shocked, white-faced figures of a handcuffed Day, his sister, the priest and the sheriff as they sat around the desk in the law office, interrupted in the process of eating supper.

'Hold it!' Martin snapped as Truman leaned back in his chair, reaching for the gunbelt hung on a peg in the wall.

'You'll never get away with it!' the lawman rasped.

'They're coming out of the saloon!' Baker yelled from the front door of the bank.

'Blast 'em!' Martin snarled, not taking his eyes off the quartet at the desk. 'Crane, get the frigging money.'

Baker's Winchester cracked twice and the crowd streaming from the saloon was so thick he could not miss. Two men fell and the others fought to get back inside.

'Bob?' Corners pleaded as Crane began to stuff dollar bills into a sack. 'I'm bleedin' to death. I think . . .'

His pain-wracked eyes finally spotted the lower half of his right leg. It was leaning, almost upright, against the head of one of the unconscious guards. Droplets of bright scarlet blood dripped evenly into the unmoving man's open mouth. Corners's voice began to quake and then he gave a groan as he sank into a faint.

'You fools!' the priest accused Martin. 'You'll never get out of town.'

Martin was sober now. His head ached from too much whiskey and his ears still rang with the impact of the explosion. But as he bellied through the hole in the insubstantial wall, he forced himself to think about what the pocked-faced priest had said. Up in the hotel room the escape had seemed the easiest part of the plan. Since

Frank's Livery had burned down, the horses were corralled in a meadow behind the houses on the south west corner of August and July. The idea had been to make a run behind the buildings, parallel with the main street, cut out four horses to ride and toss sticks of dynamite amongst the rest, killing or stampeding the animals.

But now, as shots began to explode from The Gates of Heaven, pouring lead into the blast-blackened bank, Martin had a better idea.

'Through the hole?' he yelled as he straightened up inside the law office.

Crane was the first to answer the call, crawling through and dragging the bulky sack of money behind him. 'Reckon I got most of it, Bob,' he said gleefully, the intoxication of so much money substituting for the lost effects of the whiskey.

'What about Corners?' Baker asked as he came through, his Winchester still smoking.

'He took his chance with the rest of us,' Martin snarled.

'My goodness,' Elizabeth exclaimed, finding her voice for the first time since the explosion had rocked the building.

Her brother took her hands in his and tried to stop them shaking. Truman stared at the self-satisfied smirk which spread across the face of Martin and cursed the penny-pinching town council that had decided there was no necessity to build a reinforced wall between the bank and the law office.

'What now?' Baker wanted to know.

Martin nodded to the quartet seated around the desk with the remains of their suppers before them. 'Forget the guy with the cuffs on,' he said easily. 'But figure out the other three. A pretty woman, a lawman and a priest. We got us a perfect set of hostages.'

'For the citizens of Summer perhaps,' the priest said ominously, raising his voice to be heard above the rattle of gunfire that was pouring into the ruined bank. 'But to those men in the den of vice across the Circle all life is cheap.'

The priest had voiced an obvious truth and the man in

The Gates of Heaven who undoubtedly had the lowest regard for human life – if his interests were involved – was organising the angry rabble into an improvised attacking force.

Calling upon his many years of army command, Haven was able to dismiss his initial urge to anger when news of the bank robbery was brought to him. So that when he descended the stairway into the saloon his time-worn face was set in an expression of cold determination and his mind was working like a well-oiled machine. He halted at a half-way point for a few moments, surveying the backs of the men crowded into doorways and at the windows as they fired wildly towards the bank. Then he looked at the stiffly angry figure of Millie Pitt as she marshalled her excited girls and ordered them to the safety of their rooms. The whores voiced their disappointment as they obeyed the Pitt's command and filed up the stairs, brushing past the tall figure in the neck brace.

'Wondered when you'd show up,' Jonas Pike called to Haven as Mann scurried nervously in the wake of complaining women.

The doctor turned bounty-hunter was sitting on the edge of a roulette table, idly spinning the wheel.

'You don't seem worried that the reward money is being stolen,' Haven replied stonily as he continued down the stairs.

Pike shrugged. 'I checked on you, Colonel,' he said, shouting to be heard above the gunfire. 'Your father left you enough money to put up ten rewards of that size.'

Haven nodded. 'I always took you for a methodical man.'

'I need to make a lot of money,' Pike answered. 'I can't afford to take chances.' He spun the wheel. 'So I check. Nothing at face value.'

Haven gave another of his restricted nods. 'Get their attention, please?' he asked.

'You'll pay damages?' Pike asked, taking the Remington from his pocket.

'Yes.'

Pike aimed and fired. The bartender at one of the curved

100

counters yelled and ducked as the mirror behind him shattered. The shooting ceased abruptly as the men turned from doors and windows, startled.

Haven addressed himself to Pike, but his words were meant for every ear in the saloon. 'If you really know me, sir, you'll be aware that irrespective of what I have left, I will allow no man to steal anything that is mine.'

'You can afford the ideal,' Pike replied.

'Precisely,' Haven agreed. 'I therefore offer –'

'Hey, you over at the saloon!' The voice of Martin cut across what the Colonel was saying and drew the attention of the men away from the tall man in the neck brace. 'You hear?'

'We hear!' a gimlet-eyed heavyweight answered from a window.

'We want safe passage out of this town,' Martin demanded.

'Up your back one!' the saloon's spokesman hurled in retort.

'Hell, they're in the sheriff's office!' a man exclaimed.

'We got tickets,' Martin shouted. 'Four of 'em. A padre, the sheriff, and a brother and sister name of Day.'

Pike reacted sharply to the boast. He straightened up from the gambling table and fixed Haven with a hard-eyed stare. 'Forget what you had in mind, mister,' he rasped.

Haven held the steady, menacing gaze. 'Don't tell me how to plan an attack,' he snapped, then turned towards the men as his fierce tone attracted their attention again. 'The offer is two hundred and fifty dollars a head on the men who robbed the bank.'

'How much for each innocent victim?' Pike rasped.

'Innocent people die every day,' Haven tossed at Pike, then started across to the front of the saloon. 'Best to split up into small groups and encircle them.'

'I'm for rushing them,' the bulky man with the gimlet eyes hissed. 'It worked for that guy Edge down the street.'

As the men used time in arguing tactics while Haven stood tacitly by, Pike moved quickly and silently towards one of the doorways which gave on to September Street.

Lights showed from houses on both sides of the street, but the occupants stayed fearfully in the doorways and on the stoops, craning to see what was happening but unwilling to risk being caught in crossfire. The more nervous ducked back inside and slammed their doors as Pike emerged from the saloon and walked quickly towards the Circle, the long coat flapping around his legs.

'What about it?' Martin demanded impatiently. 'We'll come out behind the hostages and you guys'll hold your fire.'

'Just try it,' a voice bellowed from the saloon and a burst of rifle and pistol fire added substance to the warning.

A man cried out and a woman screamed. Pike was on the run, taking advantage of the gunfire and crash of shattered glass to angle across the Circle to the bullet scarred bank. But he knew it was Elizabeth who had screamed and the knowledge drove him to greater speed. He reached the opposite sidewalk and pulled up sharply as the covering noise ceased.

'John!' Elizabeth said shrilly.

'You hit the Day guy!' Martin yelled. 'You stupid lunkheads.'

Elizabeth began to sob.

Pike went on to the balls of his feet to step through the shattered doorway into the bank. He saw a movement in the rear of the room and jerked up the Remington as he went into a crouch. Edge, moving in through the rear doorway, snapped the Winchester up to the aim and whirled sideways on. Neither man could clearly see the other but both sensed an identification a moment before their fingers moved the final fraction of an inch against their triggers.

The atmosphere was rancid with burnt powder and fresh blood. Each had to step over the bullet-riddled bodies of the Pinkerton men, and met beside the dead, mutilated form of Corners. Light shafted into the room through the hole in the wall. Edge reached it first and squatted down to peer through as a renewed burst of firing came from the saloon.

He saw the three bank raiders crouching below the window sill, as bullets whistled over their heads to smash into the walls of the office. Two of them were facing the window and rose to pump shots across the street. The third was covering the hostages, who lay full-length on the floor. The priest was praying, moving his lips silently. Sheriff Truman looked with a fixed stare towards his out-of-reach gun on the peg. Elizabeth was sobbing as she cradled John's head to her breast, unmindful of the river of blood that pumped from a gaping wound in his throat to form a broadening stain on her jacket. As Edge watched, the young man gurgled up a final bubbling spring of blood and then sighed into death.

Elizabeth shrieked her grief.

'The whole frigging lot are coming at us!' Baker yelled and opened up with his rifle.

'Hostages no damn good!' Crane croaked, close to tears as he began to fire.

Elizabeth started to rise, her features contorted into near ugliness by hysterical grief. Martin glanced out of the window and saw men spilling from the doorways of the saloon, bringing up their weapons to the aim. The sight rooted him to the spot for a moment. Then he quaked and moved forward, reaching for the money sack on the desk.

Edge took aim and started to squeeze the trigger. Pike tugged at his coat as he tried to wriggle into the hole. The bullet was meant for Martin's heart. It seared through the reaching hand. The four fingers were sheered off and twisted across the room. Martin screamed and run for the rear door, jerking it open and disappearing. Baker and Crane emptied their guns and spun around at the sound of a shot from behind them.

'It's gone wrong!' Crane sobbed.

'Where's Bob?' Baker screamed.

'Figured it first,' Edge muttered and sent a bullet into Crane's heart as he jerked himself through the hole.

'Fire!' Haven commanded.

Elizabeth was standing at her full height, holding her head in her hands as she swayed her body. Edge lunged at her and encircled her knees with an arm as his shoulder thudded into her stomach. She screamed and toppled as a deafening fusillade of shots sounded out on the street. A hail of bullets, like Gatling gun fire, tore into the office. Up to a dozen smashed into Baker's back and head, lifting him off his feet and flinging him across the office like a piece of rag dripping red dye.

The sheriff was caught reaching up for his gunbelt and three bullets drilled neat holes through his already injured hand.

'Cease fire!' Haven's voice boomed.

There were a few seconds of silence, and then heavy footfalls sounded on the sidewalk outside. Some twenty hard-eyed stares raked the tableau of carnage presented by the office. They looked without emotion at the survivors as they got to their feet: Edge helping Elizabeth, the sheriff holding his bloodied hand to his middle, the priest with face turned heavenwards in thanks, and Pike who looked at the lean half-breed and the distraught woman with an expression of profound thought.

But then the men spotted the sack on the desk. Edge prodded it with the Winchester muzzle and it tipped, spilling a mixture of money and dynamite sticks on to the blood-stained floor. Greedy smiles spread across the faces of the men.

'Hey, where's the other one?' a man demanded. 'Corners' next door in the bank and these dead 'uns are Baker and Crane. They all been hanging around with that Texan – Bob Martin. He was in it for sure. What happened to him?'

Edge urged the woman towards the front door of the office, keeping himself between her and the body of her dead brother. The priest fell in behind him.

'You see another of 'em, Mr Edge?' a man asked. 'Was Bob Martin here?'

The men fell back to allow Edge and the others to pass through on to the street.

'Yeah,' the half breed answered. 'He was here. But he took a powder.'

CHAPTER TWELVE

SUDDEN death was no stranger to the men who had rained it upon the law office and even as the town's overworked undertaker was still making arrangements for the bodies to be removed The Gates of Heaven began to resound with music, shouting and laughter again. On the quiet streets away from the aura of light and noise radiated by Solar Circle, the citizens of the town retired for the night. There had been another shooting, but lately such incidents had become commonplace. It was nothing to stay awake worrying about.

Edge took Elizabeth Day to the church house and the priest's wife – deeply shocked herself that the supper she had cooked for John Day should have caused her husband to become a hostage – attended to putting the bereaved woman to bed. Pike came to the house a few minutes later, carrying a valise filled with medical instruments and medicine bottles.

He saw Edge and the priest in the sitting room of the small, neat house and was intrigued by the attitude of interrogation which the half breed was adopting. But he went up the stairs and gave a sedative to Elizabeth before giving in to his curiosity. When he finally entered the sitting room, the priest was alone.

A horse snorted out at the back of the house, then hoofbeats sounded. The animal trotted across Solar Circle and was heeled into a gallop down August towards the bridge.

'Edge?' Pike asked the priest.

The man nodded, the smallpox scars on his pale face very pronounced in the flickering lamp light. 'He asked to borrow it.'

'He's not the kind of man to ask for favours,' Pike said thoughtfully.

'Not normally,' the priest agreed. 'But he seems to have

105

changed somewhat tonight.'

'It's what makes the world go round, padre,' Pike said. 'But he's still got a yen for the money?' He showed his crooked smile. 'Two can't live as cheaply as one.'

'He was asking me about the family of one of the men he killed at the newspaper office. Bradford Rivers. Oddly enough, another ... another man was asking the same questions a few days ago.'

'Man named Silas Hyman?' Pike suggested.

The priest was surprised. 'How did you know?' he asked.

Pike held on to the smile. 'I make it my business to know things,' he replied. 'I'd appreciate it if you'd tell me what you told Edge.'

The priest nodded. 'Why not. The sooner somebody finds Haven's belongings and collects the reward the better it will be for Summer.'

It didn't take long to tell and less than fifteen minutes had past since Edge had crossed the bridge when Pike rode his horse out of the corral and galloped in pursuit of the half-breed.

The Chandler farmstead was small and ill cared for. It was ten miles east of Summer, reached by a spur which left the stage trail and took a tortuous, twisting route among foothills country. Edge slowed the horse to a walk when he came within sight of the spread and halted at the leaning gate to the yard. His hooded eyes focused upon the single lighted window in the delapidated, one-storey house then roved over the two small barns. There was an empty corral behind one of the barns and the house and its out-buildings were surrounded on three sides by neatly tilled fields. It was all clearly defined in the frosty moonlight.

The tall, lean half-breed turned in the saddle and saw a narrow gully that offered a hiding place for the horse. He dismounted and led the animal out of sight from the track, where he tethered it. He left the saddle in place but slid the Winchester from the forward hung boot. Then he returned to the open gate of the Chandler farm and followed the fence around to the barn with the corral behind it.

He found a split board to peer through and enough moonlight shafted in through holes in the roof to show him the barn was empty. It smelled of rotting timber and decomposing animal feed. He moved quickly and silently to the second barn which looked from the outside to be in as bad a state of repair as the first, unpainted and apparently holed in many places. But Edge could see nothing as he tried to peer inside and when he prodded at the holes with the Winchester he discovered they had been repaired from the inside. There was a heavy padlock holding the two big doors at the front firmly closed.

He eyed the lock for a few moments, then shook his head and turned to lope silently across to the house. It was little more than a four roomed shack, its timbers warped and with several broken panes of glass replaced by balled up newspaper.

He looked through the lighted window into the living room. It was sparsely furnished with a whitewood table, two ladderback chairs and a bureau poorly stocked with unmatching china. There was no fire in the grate and the light was shed by an unshaded lamp hung from the centre of the blackened ceiling.

Two coffins, plain pine and open, rested across the table. The pale, stiff faces of Bradford Rivers and Frank Chandler showed above the starched whiteness of their burial robes. A woman in her seventies, with skin like dirty parchment and eyes that looked dead, sat in one of the chairs in silent vigil. She held an empty shot glass in one hand and a half full bottle of whiskey in the other. Her movements, as she filled the glass, lifted it to her lips and swallowed the amber liquid in one were almost mechanical. Her lips moved, perhaps in prayer, perhaps counting the seconds, and then she took another drink.

Edge, his expression impassive, reached the door on the balls of his feet. There was no way of telling whether or not it was locked. He stepped back, raised a leg and thrust the heel of his boot against the door. It whipped open and crashed back against the wall. He followed it in, the Winchester levelled.

The old woman looked up without surprise, and fixed

Edge with a vacant stare. 'My last kin are dead,' she said in a croaky voice. 'My nephew Frank and his brother-in-law. I'm alone in the world now.'

She went through the jerky series of movements that led to her taking a drink. Edge felt the intense cold of the room – worse than outside. And smelt the evil fragrance of cheap whiskey and the unwashed body of the women. He moved around to each of the three doors leading off the living room. Two gave on to bare boards and walls. A third opened to show him a rancid kitchen with an evil-smelling mattress on the floor in one corner. Whiskey bottles, some full but most empty, littered the room.

'You farm the place yourself?' Edge asked, recalling the well-tended fields and the patched up barn.

'Frank sent out men,' she croaked. 'He was a good boy.' She took a shot. 'More like a son than a nephew. Made sure I always had plenty of medicine.' She held up the bottle.

'Rich man, uh?' Edge asked, leaning against the door-frame, able to watch the approach to the farm and to breath in the cold, fresh air from outside.

The old woman nodded. 'Did well for himself in Summer. Owned the Last Rose restaurant and the livery. Few stores as well. Now he's dead and it's all over.'

'How'd he get to be so rich?' Edge wanted to know as he cradled the Winchester in the crook of his arm and took out the makings.

'He had friends that helped him. Just to get started. But he repaid them, many times over.'

Edge nodded. 'Real couple of swingers,' he muttered.

The old lady took a drink. 'I didn't catch that?'

'The Balls,' Edge supplemented as he lit the cigarette.

The crone narrowed her eyes and a mild suspicion was injected into them. But then she shrugged her thin shoulders. 'Don't matter now Frank's dead. Nobody's supposed to know about Frank and Brad supplying the Ball boys and their men.' She sighed. 'Mr Bolan's due in with the wagon tonight. I'll have to tell him what happened – that it's all over.'

'My condolences, ma'am,' Edge said and stepped out over the threshhold.

He returned to his horse the way he had come, moving along the line of the fence, his narrowed eyes scanning the surrounding country. But when the wagon rolled down the track towards the Chandler farm it came with a complete lack of stealth and with no advance scouts.

It figured, Edge reasoned as he stroked the horse's neck to keep the animal quiet and watched the covered wagon roll past and go through the sagging gateway. Chandler had been repaying the Balls for their backing for a long time and the farm of the drunken old lady had been a supply drop for the gang for many years. The gang had good reason to consider the arrangement a safe one.

But Silas Hyman had been close to uncovering the scheme – had perhaps seen Brad Rivers on one of his wagon trips from town, loaded with supplies drawn from Chandler's stores. Whatever had aroused his suspicion, he had questioned the priest about Rivers and been told of his relationship to Chandler and of the existence of the farm and its elderly owner.

But he had died following another lead and it wasn't until Pike mentioned the name of the liveryman that Edge realised the tortured man's final word was a name rather than a location.

Edge moved forward for a better view of the farm as the poker-faced Bolan turned the wagon and backed it up to the front of the patched barn. Then he froze, hearing a slight sound behind him. But before he could whirl and level the Winchester, the needle point of Pike's stiletto was pressed against the small of his back. It pierced his clothes and pricked the skin in the area of his kidneys. He sighed. 'What's up, doc?' he rasped softly.

'I could have killed you,' Pike hissed.

'That's what bugs me,' Edge said. 'Why didn't you?'

'Big gang,' Pike answered. 'Haven thinks six at least. Two of us makes better sense than one. Even division of labour and a like arrangement with the reward. Do we have a deal?'

Edge looked across at the farm as Bolan jumped down

from the wagon and went to the barn doors, ignoring the house. He had a key to fit the padlock and the doors swung wide.

'Seems like I'm stuck with it,' Edge growled.

Pike withdrew the knife and showed his crooked smile as the half-breed turned to look at him. 'It was just to stop you making any noise,' he said as he slid the weapon into the sheath inside his boot.

Edge's hooded eyes looked along the gully behind Pike and saw the man's horse tethered a hundred feet off. 'How many others did you lead out here?' he asked scornfully.

The smile dropped from the smaller man's face and his eyes became hard as they locked upon Edge's rebuking gaze. 'I never make the same mistake twice,' he rasped.

'Once is often enough to get a man killed,' Edge answered, turning away to survey the farm again as Bolan began to load cartons, sacks and barrels on to the wagon.

Pike moved up beside him and they watched in silence for several seconds. Then he asked: 'Supplies for the gang?'

'What do you think?'

'Know how far off they're holed up?'

Edge pursed his thin lips. 'Unless that guy drove the team hard, more than a couple of city blocks. His horses are pretty beat.'

'He doesn't intend to rest them,' Pike pointed out as Bolan closed and locked the barn doors then hurried to the front of the wagon and hoisted himself up on to the seat.

'All done, Annie!' Bolan yelled, his voice carrying clearly through the night silence to where Edge and Pike were hidden.

'It's all over,' the old woman responded from inside the rancid house, her voice thick with too much whiskey.

'Yeah,' Bolan answered, reading a question into her words. 'Be back in a couple of months.'

He slapped the reins against the team and the wagon jerked forward into a wide turn which took it through the gateway on to the trail. The old crone shouted something, but it was lost amid the stamp of hooves and rumble of wheels. She staggered out through the open door and sagged against the frame as she saw the wagon rolling away from her. She lifted the bottle in a beckoning gesture, but then shrugged and poured herself another drink. She took it at a gulp and shuffled back inside.

'Let's go,' Edge said as the wagon trundled past on the track and he swung up on to his horse.

'I'll be right behind you,' Pike answered, turning to head back towards his own mount.

'Good place to be when the shooting starts,' Edge muttered.

CHAPTER THIRTEEN

BOLAN had not driven the wagon team hard on the trip to the farm. It was a long haul from the hide-out which the gang called the ballpark to their supply point and the route lay across rugged terrain.

Bolan, unaware of the two men on his trail, left the rutted spur road and angled northwards, deep into the heart of the barren foothills. There was no clearly defined track to follow and he steered the wagon team by landmarks memorised from many previous trips.

Because the horses were already wearied by the outward trip the going was slow, through narrow ravines and along the floors of broad valleys; crossing shallow streams and by-passing deeper, more turbulent water courses.

As the heavily laden wagon creaked higher into the hills and the night reached towards a new day, it got colder. Expelled air from the lungs of men and animals showed up as white plumes of mist against the deep shadows cast by cliffs and outcrops in the silvery moonglow.

Then, as the temperatures plunged lower, the false dawn splashed greyness across the eastern sky. A few snowflakes drifted ineffectually down and the unsuspecting Bolan and his pursuers saw the higher range of mountains ahead of them, coated with the dark green vegetation that gave the Black Hills their name.

The inclines steepened, slowing progress still further and it was full dawn, with a cold red sun clear of the horizon when Bolan brought the team around into a turn, angling towards a stand of lush pine trees. He steered the team along a natural track among the trees and died just as he was about to enter a narrow ravine.

The two Teton Dakota braves had been poised on the lower branches of trees which flanked the entrance to the ravine. They could see each other through the scented foliage and used hand signals to start their attack.

Bolan heard a gentle swishing sound and looked up in alarm. Horror sprang into his eyes and he fumbled with the buttons of his heavy coat, vainly trying to reach his Colt. But he knew instantly that he would fail and his mouth opened to start a scream.

The brave who dropped on to the seat on the left gave a savage thrust with his knife, burying it to the hilt in the white man's chest. The scream emerged as a pained gasp and then the brave on the right swung his tomahawk. As the first brave withdrew his knife to undam a spout of arterial blood, the curved blade of the decorated hatchet sliced through the flesh and bone of the dead man's neck. Bolan's head rolled into the rear of the wagon as his body was kicked sideways from the seat by the braves.

The brave who had used the knife grasped the reins and the second attacker lashed at the team with a bull whip. The pain of the viciously wielded leather drove a final reserve of strength into the legs of the exhausted horses and they raced down the ravine in a panicked, headlong gallop, their hoofbeats thunderously resounding off the steep walls.

Edge and Pike reined their mounts to a skidding halt as the forward surge of the wagon signalled the appearance of more than twenty Sioux riders from out of the trees. Edge whisked the Winchester from the saddle boot and Pike drew an elegantly made, ornately decorated English rifle. But neither man fired, content merely to aim their weapons at the backs of the buckskin-clad Indians until they disappeared into the ravine.

'Seems we have competition,' Pike said softly as the noise from the unshod ponies diminished.

'Indians bother you?' Edge asked easily, his eyes raking across the wooded vista for signs of stragglers.

'Not while I've got this,' Pike replied, slapping the silver embossed stock of the rifle.

Edge glanced at the rifle scornfully. 'Pretty fancy.'

'Martini-Henry,' Pike explained. 'Bought it in England.'

'You didn't have it this morning,' Edge said, satisfied that the whole party of braves had gone into the ravine and heeling his mount forward.

'Didn't think you'd be so touchy,' Pike replied easily. 'I only use this to kill people.'

'What about the blade?'

Pike showed his crooked smile. 'Like your razor, Edge. For close in stuff.'

Edge jerked the Winchester towards the headless corpse of Bolan, already stiffening in the bitter cold. 'They can get pretty close, Pike,' he warned.

'I'll take my chances,' Pike said evenly. 'I need that money.'

'I'm not doing this because I like Haven,' Edge said as they entered the ravine and heard a burst of gunfire ahead.

'Nor only for yourself anymore,' Pike answered.

Edge stared hard at Pike as they rode, side by side, holding their horses down to a walk. 'She tell you why she took it into her head to make a try for the reward?' he asked.

'For her brother's defence,' Pike answered. 'Lawyers come higher than stabling or hotel rooms in Summer. No need now, though.'

The gunfire channelled along the ravine between the high walls was now interspersed with warcries as the Sioux closed on their target.

'I've still got reason to want it,' Edge said.

He dug in his heels and the horse leapt forward as if anxious to get to the scene of the shooting. Pike urged his mount into a gallop only inches to the rear.

The ravine, cold and shadowed by its walls, opened out suddenly into the ballpark. This was a broad area of grass-land surrounded by ragged ridged hills, like enormous prehistoric animals at rest. It was divided into two un-equal sections by a ten feet wide river running east to west and as Edge and Pike emerged into the sunlight the Sioux raiders were on the point of rushing into the water behind the hi-jacked wagon.

Two hundred feet back from the far bank was a towering tongue of yellow sandstone that curled away from a hill like a crescent-shaped promontory in a dried up ocean. The face of the rock was pocked with dozens of caves and it was from one of the larger openings that answering fire was directed at the attacking Indians. The mouth of the cave was flanked by two wagons identical to the one that now splashed clear of the river and angled away from the defenders' guns.

The gang's horses, which had been grazing in a loose group some way from the cave mouth, snorted at the gun-shots and bolted, streaming into the crossfire. Two of the panicked animals took bullets in their chests and rolled, sliding across the frosted ground into the path of the wagon team. The horses in the shafts veered sharply to the side and the wagon tipped, tossing the two braves clear. One of them thudded to the ground with such force that the wooden handle of his tomahawk burst into his stomach to spill the first Indian blood of the attack.

His companion landed on his feet but the impact broke both his legs and the brilliant white of jagged thighbones ripped through his flesh and leggings. The brave turned his knife against himself but a shot into his heart killed him before he could cut his throat. His chief, who had fired the fatal shot, spat on the dead brave as he leapt his pony over the sprawled form. Then he screamed a shrill battlecry and led his braves in a vee formation towards the cave mouth, raining a hail of lead at the opening.

One brave, whirling a scalp decorated lance, saw Bolan's severed head among the debris scattered by the overturned wagon and broke away from the attack. The point of the lance stabbed into raw meat of the neck and the brave whooped with delight as he thrust the lance skywards with his gruesome prize.

'Bastards got Bolan!' Ed Ball bellowed as he crouched in the cave mouth, the Winchester bucking in his hands. His fleshy face wore a mask of horror and his obese frame was trembling, spoiling his aim.

Beside him, his elder brother was less moved by the bloodied head atop the lance than by the fierce-faced line of Indians pounding towards him. 'Serves him right for leading them here,' he rasped, taking careful aim and lifting three braves from their ponies with six shots.

Kelton, Bean and Lambert were prone on the dusty ground in the cave, firing wildly with two Springfields and a Winchester. Bullets whistled over their heads to chip at the rock inside the cave, or kicked up spurts of dirt around their bodies. A shot from Kelton gouged into the eye of a pony and its rider leapt clear and started to run. Bean and Lambert fired at the same time and the top of the brave's head exploded with a surge of blood and bone fragments.

The gunfire, echoing off the walls of the cave, was deafening, drowning out the whoops and cries of the attackers. Nobody heard Pete Bean scream as a bullet ploughed a furrow across his forehead. But the injured man's blood sprayed into the face of Kelton, who looked around in anger and took two bullets in the cheek. Two more Indians were blasted from their ponies by shots from the brothers as the chief veered away less than twenty feet from the cave mouth.

The lance carrier flicked his weapon and Bolan's head bounced against the hard ground and rolled into the cave mouth. Lambert saw it coming towards him and scrambled on to all fours to get away from it. The lance swished through the gunsmoke thickened air and penetrated the man's chest. He screamed and toppled backwards, struggling to pull the weapon free. But it burst out of his back with a gush of blood and ripped flesh. His dead body was impaled against the ground.

'They're leaving!' Ed cried in trembling delight, a harsh

laugh spilling through his thick lips as he hauled himself upright.

'They'll be back,' Tom said coldly as he watched the braves ride out of rifle range, then scanned the area in front of the cave. He counted a half dozen Sioux dead, then surveyed the men in the cave. Ed was unhurt, but his heavily fleshed body was still gripped by a fit of trembling that could signal hysteria. Lambert was dead. Kelton soon would be as he groaned away his strength, blood from the awful wounds in his face pumping out to form a pool in which his dislodged right eye was floating. The whole of Bean's head and front of his shirt were soaked with blood from his forehead wound. But he was conscious.

'Let the bastards take what they want!' Bean pleaded, trying to stem the flow of blood with one hand as he wiped at his eyes with the other.

'All they want is us,' Tom growled, feeding shells into his Springfield as he peered out at the Indians. They were gathered in a group around the chief, listening to what he was saying but looking with piercing eyes towards the cave mouth. 'Won't be satisfied with nothing less.'

Bean stared hatefully at Ed. 'It's his fault,' he snarled, pointing an accusing finger. 'Sioux didn't get stirred up 'til after we hit that army train and Haven brought in the bounty hunters. It's all those saddletramps on Sioux land that put them on the warpath. And for what?'

Ed's small eyes gleamed dangerously through their layers of fat. 'Didn't hear you complaining none at how we been living!' he bellowed.

A full-throated warcry captured the men's attention and they whirled to see the braves bearing down upon them again, a fusillade of arrows backing up the hail of lead that was directed at the cave.

'Get them inside!' Tom barked, pumping off two shots before backing away into the depths of the cave.

The others did not hold back, but scrambled after the elder Ball brother without firing at the galloping braves. There were three tunnels leading out of the cave and the trio went into the centre one, disappearing from sight a moment before the leading brave sprang from his racing pony and ran into the shadowed interior. The others were only moments behind him, hitting the ground lightly, balanced, with rifles and bows at the ready.

Disappointment rumbled in their throats and their paint-daubed faces were contorted by anger. Then the chief saw the tunnels at the rear of the cave and emitted a triumphant roar. A trail of blood from Beans' forehead wound showed which way the white men had gone.

Kelton, hovering on the edge of consciousness, saw his discarded rifle with his good eye. His hand inched forward towards the stock. A bow string was released and Kelton screamed. His hand was pinned to the ground by an arrow.

'Scalps?' a brave said in English and the chief nodded.

Kelton screamed his last as a knife slashed along his hair line and a hand tugged at the trophy. The entire top of his head became a pulpy mass of bubbling blood as the hirsuite skin was torn free. Another brave claimed the scalp of Lambert and a third held Bolan's head as a fourth peeled off the topknot.

Then the whole party streamed into the centre tunnel with the chief in the lead.

Edge and Pike waited until all trace of movement had gone from the cave mouth before they galloped out into the open. They demanded every last ounce of power from their horses as they raced for the river, splashed through the slow flowing water and up the far bank. Without pre-planning, Edge went to the left of the cave and Pike to the right, skidding their mounts to a halt behind the parked wagons.

Rifle fire sounded, far off in the depths of the cave-riddled sandstone, as they tied the animals to the wagons. The Indian ponies stamped nervously and snorted, but stayed in a close group. There were fourteen of them.

'That fancy rifle got a fast action?' Edge called to Pike, and nodded to the ponies.

'All of them?' the smaller man asked as he slid the Martini-Henry from the saddle boot.

Edge shrugged. 'Just one of those redskins get away and

we might have to fight the whole Sioux nation to get back to town.'

Pike nodded. Then, with a fluid, incredibly fast movement, he brought the stock of the rifle to his shoulder and began to fire and work the lever action. Before Edge could unboot his Winchester, four of the ponies were on their sides, pumping blood from neat bullet holes between their eyes. The other animals reared and kicked in their panic to get clear of the group as more of their number tumbled under the hail of lead from smoking rifles.

Six broke away unharmed and galloped for the river in blind terror. Edge lowered his rifle and began to feed fresh rounds into the breech as he watched Pike continue to fire. The small man in the long coat placed his shots with cool speed and not one was wasted. The sixth horse died on the river bank and pitched into the water.

'You ain't bad,' Edge allowed evenly as Pike began to reload his rifle. Then added: 'At shooting horses.'

'There has to be a good reason to use it on people,' Pike answered. 'But it shoots just as straight at them.'

'So let's give it a whirl,' Edge said, striding into the cave and stepping over the mutilated bodies of Kelton and Lambert.

'Once more into the breech, dear friend,' Pike misquoted as he fed the final bullet into the rifle.

'Quit sweet-talking the Martini and shake it up,' Edge growled over his shoulder, stepping towards the tunnel entrance.

CHAPTER FOURTEEN

THREE braves who had heard the shooting from outside the cave emerged at the tunnel mouth and hesitated a fatal second as they saw Edge and Pike bearing down upon them.

Edge shot away the jaw of one and he fell writhing to the ground. Pike drilled a bullet through the heart of another. As the enraged brave in the centre drew back an arm to hurl his tomahawk, the two white men fired together and the Indian clutched at the twin spouts of blood gushing from his stomach.

Edge drew his razor in a blur of hand and arm movement and Pike slid out the stiletto as he bobbed into a crouch and straightened. The two braves who had not died under the rifle fire stared up in terror as the white men approached. Razor and knife slashed under their outstretched arms and the Indians choked on their own blood as gaping wounds were opened in their throats.

Edge and Pike leapt across the blood-drenched bodies of the Indians and broke into a run along the tunnel. There was a continuous barrage of rifle fire now, as each report was echoed and re-echoed along the rock walls. They raced around a turn and pulled up sharply, peering through the drifting gunsmoke at the lamp-lit scene before them.

The tunnel gave entrance to a large cavern with a high, vaulted roof and smooth, yellow-tinted walls. The floor, where it showed, was of hard-packed clay. But for the most part it was covered by elaborately patterned Persian carpets. On the carpets stood English and French furniture – a four-poster canopied bed, a circular rosewood table with accompanying high-backed chairs, a mirrored chest of drawers, an oak desk, a glass-fronted bookcase with leather-bound volumes lining the shelves – even an enamel bath-tub. On the furniture and on the floor there was a fortune in crystal, china and silver. Leaning against the walls or resting upon natural niches in them were many gilt-framed land-scapes and portraits – including one of Haven in a Colonel's uniform – done in oils. The heavily ornamented lamps glowed with the dull sheen of unpolished silver.

Pike gave a low whistle as he took in the incongruous luxury of the cave dwelling. 'Haven's got taste,' he murmured, and dived flat to the ground as a riccocheting bullet tugged at his coat sleeve. The Martini bucked in his hands and the bullet blew open the back of a brave's head.

Edge's lips curled back into a scornful sneer as his eyes raked over the cave's elaborate furnishing. 'My army was never like this,' he muttered, spotting the Ball brothers and Bean pinned down behind a hastily erected barricade of a sofa and three wing chairs in one corner.

The Sioux braves were spread out across the cave in a half circle, using the stoutly made furniture as cover. Glass shattered and wood splintered at each crack of a rifle. Two Indians had been killed before Edge and Pike reached the inner cave and now three more died as the newcomers blasted at the exposed braves.

An Indian climbed on to the bed canopy and fired an arrow across the top of the pile of chairs. It made a peculiar sucking noise as it entered Bean's right eye and pierced his brain.

Ed Ball, tears of fear stinging his eyes, every muscle in his obese frame quivering, launched himself forward, leaping over the barricade, screaming at the top of his voice and firing as he ran. A volley of shots rattled and the fat youngster's face disappeared in welter of cascading blood.

The brave on the bed canopy took a bullet in the leg and another in the heart as he tumbled. Tom Ball, his coolness unaffected by what had happened to his brother, waited for the braves to be panicked by the crossfire then placed his shots as they broke cover. Edge, in a half crouch and Pike, still prone on the ground, aimed at the terrified braves with professional accuracy, dropping a man with every shot.

The pattern on the high-priced carpet became obliterated by dark stains of blood and pieces of sopping flesh rained down upon the beautiful furniture.

'I think they've had enough,' Edge rasped as he, Pike and Tom Ball fired together, the three bullets ripping into the flesh of the Sioux chief and blasting him backwards into the bathtub. His blood dripped through the unplugged drainaway.

'There aren't any more redskins,' Pike pointed out, getting slowly to his feet and scanning the litter of bodies scattered among the luxurious furnishings.

'So they've had enough,' Edge answered with a shrug,

covering Tom Ball with the Winchester. His hooded eyes met and held the other man's cold gaze. 'How about you, feller?'

Ball hesitated, then sighed and tossed his rifle to the ground as he came out from behind the bullet-holed barricade. 'Me, too,' he answered, unbuckling his gunbelt and letting it fall. Sadness entered his eyes as he looked down at the bloodied body of his brother. 'You got us into one hell of a mess, Ed,' he accused softly.

'And he's left it to you to get the mess out,' Edge told him. He jerked a thumb towards the tunnel. 'All this junk, on the wagons.'

Anger flared in the green eyes. 'On my own?'

Edge glanced quizzically at Pike. 'You want to help him, doc?'

Pike showed his crooked smile. 'We saved his life. I don't think he should expect anything else from us.'

'Except that we shouldn't take it away from him,' Edge said, raising the Winchester so that Ball was looking straight into the muzzle.

Ball's shoulders drooped in submission. Then he swung towards the nearest piece of furniture – one of the upended chairs – and lifted it.

Edge and Pike took turns in escorting him along the tunnel with his burdens and he was allowed to halt only when the bulk of a particular item meant it had to be dismantled so that he could carry it. The removal took up the rest of the morning and was not completed until midway into the afternoon. The smell of death in the inner cavern and at the mouth of the cave grew thicker and more cloying with each minute that passed.

Following instructions from Edge, Ball harnessed the saddle horses into the shafts of the wagon. Edge climbed up on to the seat of one and Pike boarded the other.

'What about me?' Ball demanded as he stood between the two wagons, breathing in deeply of the cold air, his face crusted by frozen sweat.

Edge finished rolling a cigarette. 'We got about as much

as these animals can haul,' he replied evenly. 'Can't take no excess.'

Ball raked his suddenly desperate eyes across the ballpark. All the Indian ponies were dead, sprawled in the frozen pools of their own blood. The team that had struggled clear of the overturned supply wagon had galloped off in terror and was unlikely to return for as long as the smell of death hovered in the frosty air. And that would be for a long time.

'Take me with you?' Ball implored. 'I'd rather hang than be left alone out here.'

Edge spat over the side of the wagon and flicked the reins to urge the horse forward. 'You heard me, feller,' he said coldly.

Ball whirled towards Pike. 'Please, mister?' he pleaded.

'Leave him!' Edge snarled, and Pike's head snapped around.

He saw the Winchester resting across the half-breed's knees, pointing at him. One olive-skinned hand was curled around the rifle and he knew a finger was resting against the trigger.

'Seems I'm not making the decisions,' he said, and clucked his horse into motion.

Ball stayed rooted to the spot as the wagons rumbled away from him. Then he saw the rifles dropped by those braves who had been killed before they reached the cave. He side-stepped towards one of them, keeping his eyes focused on the departing wagons. But as he stooped to pick up the weapon, a shot rang out. He was flipped over on to his back, blood blossoming across his chest.

Edge straightened up on the seat and rested the smoking Winchester against the brake lever. A satisfied smile curled up the corners of his thin mouth as he arced the cigarette stub into the river.

'You knew he'd make a try,' Pike accused.

Edge shrugged. 'I didn't need him anymore, but I needed him to give me a reason.'

Pike stared hard at Edge, his mind searching for an explanation of such a man who dealt out death so lightly

122

and yet only killed by the rules of his own moral code. Then they reached the narrow ravine which provided the only exit from the ballpark and the wagons had to get into line to pass through. Edge took his to the front and that was where he stayed for the rest of that day and through the night. And Pike felt happier to be the back marker on the long, slow journey to Summer. For he had a suspicion that the half-breed might consider the opportunity to claim the entire reward as sufficient justification to kill him.

But, for his part, Edge gave no thought to the man on the wagon behind him. Pike had earned his half of Haven's reward money and Edge had learned enough about human nature to recognise those men he could trust and those he could not. So the tall, lean half-breed allowed his mind to wander ahead, across the lonely hills, to consider the grief-stricken Elizabeth Day. But at times this train of thought was interrupted and his mind travelled backwards in time, recalling another woman. Her name had been Jeannie* and as he thought about her his hooded eyes showed an expression close to sadness. For she had been the only human being he had loved outside of his family, And now, a violent, blood-soaked eternity after Jeannie had died, Edge tried to discover whether his feelings towards Elizabeth went deep enough to be termed love.

He could not answer the question and justified the failure by telling himself that a brain could not be expected to function properly after two days and two nights without sleep. But when he drove the wagon across the rattling bridge and along August Street in the frosty sunlight of morning, he found his answer in the sight of the woman.

She was standing in front of the stage line office, dressed entirely in borrowed black, her pretty face pale and drawn. Millie Pitt and Mann flanked her as if waiting to catch her if she fell.

As Edge and Pike angled the wagons across the street and reined in the exhausted saddle horses, The Gates of Heaven spilled out its clutch of drifters and bounty hunters. They blinked in the sunlight and then a rumble of dis-

*See: *Edge – Killer's Breed.*

content ran through the group as they realised what the wagons contained.

But they kept their curses low-keyed and made no forward move as Edge and Pike dropped to the ground, rifles held loosely in their hands.

'Heading for home, Miss Day?' Pike asked, touching his hat.

She shook her head sadly. 'With Byron and John both dead, I have no home. Miss Pitt says there's plenty of work for a seamstress in Deadwood.'

Pike nodded and looked into the stubbled face of Edge. 'How about you, Edge?' he asked.

'My business,' the half-breed muttered, bringing up the rifle as a man burst through the line of watchers in front of the saloon.

But he eased his grip as he recognised the military figure of Haven. The man was carrying a valise and from the avaricious glints in the eyes of the watchers, Edge knew it contained the reward money.

'You've got it?' Haven demanded in high excitement, striding to peer into the rear of the first wagon.

'Little the worse for wear, but we got it,' Edge answered.

Haven gasped. 'My God, it's covered in blood!'

Pike stared levelly at the half-breed. 'It's the way things have to be in Edge's book,' he said softly.

'But let's make that enough for this one,' the half-breed rasped, bringing the Winchester to bear on Haven. 'You made the deal – no strings.'

Haven regained his composure and held out the valise. 'I did, and I do not welch. This can all be restored. Who wants the money?'

'Fifty-fifty?' Pike said.

Edge nodded. 'I'll count it.'

He took the valise and rested it on the sidewalk. The men in front of the saloon surged forward, but pulled up short as Pike's ornate rifle swung along the line. Edge snapped open the valise and Mann gasped at the sight of the money.

Then Millie Pitt touched Edge on the shoulder as he began to count out the bills. 'Don't suppose you want to buy a hotel, mister?' she asked.

Edge ignored her and she looked questioningly at Pike. The man in the long coat showed her his crooked smile and shook his head. 'It's going to be rather short on guests after today,' he pointed out.

'Bad buy,' Mann agreed.

'Nobody asked you, pint size!' the madam snarled, and lashed out at the drummer, slapping him across the cheek.

Edge, his calculations completed, stood up and began to push his share of the money into his pockets as Mann massaged his stinging cheek, staring malevolently at the madam. Sheriff Truman, his hand heavily bandaged, appeared in the doorway of the stage line office. His eyes poured hatred on Edge.

'Where were you when the Pitt hit the Mann?' the half-breed asked.

'Checking if there's a spare seat on the stage,' the lawman hissed. 'There is, if you want it.'

Edge held the steady stare of hate for a few moments, then glanced at Pike. 'What about you, doc?' he asked as the smaller man stooped and picked up the valise.

'What I need this money for is in the opposite direction,' he said cryptically.

Edge avoided looking at Elizabeth as he held out a bill towards Truman. 'Buy me a ticket, sheriff,' he said.

Truman grinned mirthlessly as he took the bill. 'My pleasure.'

'Better hurry it up,' the Pitt urged, looking over the heads of the men in front of her hotel, towards the high ground behind the town. 'The Deadwood Stage is a comin' on over the hill.'

Now Edge's hooded eyes met Elizabeth's blank expression. 'Mind if I ride along with you, Miss Day?' he asked.

'For goodness sake, you're free to do as you please,' she answered, and cast her eyes down to the ground.

'Looks like someone's got a secret love,' the Pitt murmured as the stage rattled along August and scattered the men in front of the saloon.

Pike stepped down from the sidewalk to cross towards the church house. 'Goodbye, Miss Day,' he said, touching his hat. 'Perhaps we'll run into each other again some time.'

His eyes met those of Edge for an instant before he turned his back on the group.

'Whatever will be, will be,' Edge muttered as the stage pulled in, blocking his view of the small man in the long coat.

THE END

NEL BESTSELLERS

T011 682	ESCAPE ON VENUS	Edgar Rice Burroughs	40p
T013 537	WIZARD OF VENUS	Edgar Rice Burroughs	30p
T009 696	GLORY ROAD	Robert Heinlein	40p
T010 856	THE DAY AFTER TOMORROW	Robert Heinlein	30p
T016 900	STRANGER IN A STRANGE LAND	Robert Heinlein	75p
T011 844	DUNE	Frank Herbert	75p
T012 298	DUNE MESSIAH	Frank Herbert	40p
T015 211	THE GREEN BRAIN	Frank Herbert	30p

War

T013 367	DEVIL'S GUARD	Robert Elford	50p
T013 324	THE GOOD SHEPHERD	C. S. Forester	35p
T011 755	TRAWLERS GO TO WAR	Lund & Ludlam	40p
T015 505	THE LAST VOYAGE OF GRAF SPEE	Michael Powell	30p
T015 661	JACKALS OF THE REICH	Ronald Seth	30p
T012 263	FLEET WITHOUT A FRIEND	John Vader	30p

Western

T016 994	No. 1 EDGE – THE LONER	George G. Gilman	30p
T016 986	No. 2 EDGE – TEN THOUSAND DOLLARS AMERICAN	George G. Gilman	30p
T017 613	No. 3 EDGE – APACHE DEATH	George G. Gilman	30p
T017 001	No. 4 EDGE – KILLER'S BREED	George G. Gilman	30p
T016 536	No. 5 EDGE – BLOOD ON SILVER	George G. Gilman	30p
T017 621	No. 6 EDGE – THE BLUE, THE GREY AND THE RED	George G. Gilman	30p
T014 479	No. 7 EDGE – CALIFORNIA KILLING	George G. Gilman	30p
T015 254	No. 8 EDGE – SEVEN OUT OF HELL	George G. Gilman	30p
T015 475	No. 9 EDGE – BLOODY SUMMER	George G. Gilman	30p
T015 769	No. 10 EDGE – VENGEANCE IS BLACK	George G. Gilman	30p

General

T011 763	SEX MANNERS FOR MEN	Robert Chartham	30p
W002 531	SEX MANNERS FOR ADVANCED LOVERS	Robert Chartham	25p
W002 835	SEX AND THE OVER FORTIES	Robert Chartham	30p
T010 732	THE SENSUOUS COUPLE	Dr. 'C'	25p

Mad

S004 708	VIVA MAD!		30p
S004 676	MAD'S DON MARTIN COMES ON STRONG		30p
S004 816	MAD'S DAVE BERG LOOKS AT SICK WORLD		30p
S005 078	MADVERTISING		30p
S004 987	MAD SNAPPY ANSWERS TO STUPID QUESTIONS		30p

NEL P.O. BOX 11, FALMOUTH, TR10 9EN, CORNWALL
Please send cheque or postal order. Allow 10p to cover postage and packing on one book plus 4p for each additional book.

Name ....

Address..

....

Title ....
(SEPTEMBER)